James Clement Moffat

Alwyn

A Romance of Study

James Clement Moffat

Alwyn
A Romance of Study

ISBN/EAN: 9783337347789

Printed in Europe, USA, Canada, Australia, Japan

Cover: Foto ©Andreas Hilbeck / pixelio.de

More available books at **www.hansebooks.com**

A L W Y N :

A ROMANCE OF STUDY.

.

JAMES C. MOFFAT.

"Who will show us any good?"—Psalm iv. 6.

ANSON D. F. RANDOLPH & COMPANY,

770 Broadway, New York.

TO

The Memory of

MARY B. MOFFAT

THIS VOLUME IS DEDICATED

IN THE SPIRIT OF A

DEVOTIONAL AFFECTION.

PROLOGUE.

I.

WE welcome thee, Belovéd, back to life,
  From deepest shades and border of the grave,
The dubious and long-protracted strife
  With Death's dread angel, to destroy or save,
  Issues in victory.   His pinions wave
No longer o'er thy couch.   And as he flies,
  With all the terrors which his presence gave,
Faintly the dawn of health begins to rise
Upon thy pallid cheek and in thy brightening eyes.

II.

Again we greet thee cheerily, and move
  No more on tiptoe in thy darkened room.
Winter meanwhile has passed away.   The grove
  Has donned his Summer robes.   The gardens bloom,
  And birds flit by on glad and dazzling plume.
And life, exultant in her bright domain,
  Welcomes thee, too, and calls thee to resume
Thy wonted place within the buoyant train
Which crowns with brilliant thought the glories of her
    reign.

(5)

III.

Companion of my common cares so long,
    And fellow-traveler on the paths of lore,
I joyful hail thee, in the voice of song,
    While climbing slow from Acheronian shore,
    With topics of our fond pursuits once more—
Pursuits which did with happier days entwine,
    Ere life for us her hues autumnal wore.
Wisely my lay might public grace decline ;
But O how much to me that it should merit thine.

INVOCATION.

I.

Ye who delight to mark the unfolding mind,
   Whose bosoms throb in sympathy with all
The aspirations, cares and joys that wind
   Around the student in mysterious thrall,
   Smile on my song.   No fabled muse I call.
By inspiration of the heart alone
   My humble narrative must stand or fall.
Nor boasts it aught to common favor known,
Ambition's arts or force, on battle-field or throne.

II.

The silent changes of the spirit's life,
   Its unseen toil, its arduous flight and slow,
Passion and Reason's oft-recurring strife,
   And dreary Doubt's intolerable woe,
   Are not, alas ! the happy themes that know
The favor of the multitude, or bring
   The higher meed which critic pens bestow.
Nathless, of such I would essay to sing,
Content that kindred lives confess the truthful string.

CANTO FIRST.

ANALYSIS.

TO I.—Alwyn's early love of knowledge—Susceptibility to influences of nature—Mountain scenery—The sea—Morning among the hills—The sun—Summer noon—Atmospheric war—Light and shade—Evening in the country—Divine bounty in the adaptation of man and nature—Dawning sense of intellectual power—Friends, Norman—Among the mountains alone—Sympathy with animate nature—Forests, their effect on the religious sentiment—Outlines in landscape—Æsthetic and moral effect of mountains—Books as expository of nature—Romance of fancy—Winter—Learning to turn the materials of nature and reading to the service of fancy—First questioning of causes—Alwyn begins to despise Norman's simple Christian faith.

ALWYN:

A ROMANCE OF STUDY.

I.

WHAT recks to tell of birth and long descent?
  Is not the spirit from Jehovah sprung?
Enough that Alwyn from his childhood bent
    Him to the toils of knowledge, and among
    The free wild mountains was his fortune flung
Almost as free; and lone, and far away
    From all the bias of the babbling tongue,
His work conversed with Nature, and his play
Was o'er the learnéd page to linger night and day.

II.

Nor yet unread the old inspired page
  Of living fact writ by the hand of God,
And on its margin stamped, from age to age,
    Too oft, alas! in characters of blood,
    With record of the path which man has trod.
Nor did the heavens, with light-bespangled train,
    Of blesséd lives the unprofaned abode,
Nor yet the seasons, in their changeful reign,
Their bounty and their wrath, roll over him in vain.

III.

Yea, from the gates of childhood had he loved
  The drama ever new by Nature spread
Among the hills and woods, where he had roved
  Whither her beauties and her wonders led,
  And fondly at her bounteous bosom fed,
Ere thought had started queries for the sense,
  Or yet reflection was to feeling wed,
Unthinking of results to issue thence,
Incurring risk and toil, their own good recompense.

IV.

Where streamlets, rushing down the mountain side,
  Leap in their giddy haste from lin to lin ;
And overhanging groves, in solemn pride
  And mystic twilight, shut their chorus in
  As with a temple, where the murmuring din,
With song of birds, half plaintive and half glad,
  The worship speak of those who cannot sin,
He oft would linger till their influence had
A kindred feeling wrought, as happy and as sad.

V.

Or when the angry winds raved through the glen,
  Driving the stormy legions in their wrath,
On some high cliff, far from abodes of men,
  Would he delight to watch the tempest's path,
  As it swept on o'er mountain, lake, and strath,
With all its cloudy train in long array,
  And the wild grace which Nature's fury hath.
Till he would long to leave his form of clay,
Rise on the warring winds, and mingle with the fray.

VI.

Or where the Atlantic breaks upon the shore,
    Anon, in storm or calm might he be found,
Filling his soul with that harmonious lore
    Taught by the Ocean's everwailing sound ;
    Or gazing on the troubled billows, crowned
With snowy foam, or on the slumbering tide,
    Whose feeble surges from the coast rebound
In dreamy murmurs low ; while far and wide
It seemed in the blue sky its distant bounds to hide.

VII.

When Summer morning crowned the hills with gold,
    And stretched their lengthened shadows o'er the plain,
When early shepherd hastening to the fold,
    Or mountain ranges of his wild domain,
    Gave to the breeze his spirit-prompted strain,
'Twas to the enthusiast boy a draft of new
    And sweeter life the highest peak to gain,
Whence all the varied landscape, bursting through
The lower twilight, lay like pictures to his view :

VIII.

The effulgent orb ascending from the deep
    Of nether space, bathed in a flood of light,
The dewy uplands, which all night did weep
    His absence, now rejoicing in the might
    Of his returning, tenderly as bright,
Like gladdened Beauty smiling in her tears :
    The obscure beyond,—skirts of retreating night
'Which still upon the western verge appears,
Like half-defeated foe, yet struggling with his fears.

IX.

The snow-white mists along a hundred vales,
  Slumbering in silence by their hidden streams,
And as the invading day their rest assails,
  Slowly ascending on the advancing beams ;
  While here and there some village coppice seems
An island in the flood of fleecy cloud,
  Melting away before the warmth which teems
From yon triumphant orb, as if the proud
Earth had awoke from death and bondage of the shroud.

X.

The voice of many waters, shining rills,
  Like living things in wilful song and play,
Which, by a thousand tiny falls, the hills
  Pour down into the glens ; the ceaseless fray,
  Where adverse streams do battle for the way,
Their graver rush united, and the roar
  Of the fierce cataract, whose hoary spray
Is Nature's incense-cloud, and evermore
The distant river's dash upon its rocky shore ;

XI.

And rising with the day the sweeter notes,
  Which draw their daily being from the sun,
The lark's clear matin hymn, which downward floats,
  As if in joy from heaven already won ;
  The long complaints, which o'er the mountains run,
From fleecy flocks descending from their lair,
  And far below from labors re-begun,
The sounds of human life, rising like prayer,
Blend into sweet accord upon the throbbing air.

XII.

Father of morning, all-beholding Sun,
  Fountain of warmth and light, without thy ray
What were this earth but cold and barren stone?
  Thy glance her oceans and her streams obey.
  Vital activity pursues thy way,
From morn till even, in meek dependence led.
  Night is thy absence and thy presence day,
  The storm is but the veiling of thy head,
And every birth of earth is by thy favor fed.

XIII.

The pride of Summer is thy steady gaze
  Poured warm and loving from a genial sky;
And Winter but thy long-averted face.
  Worlds hang upon thy bounty, and with thy
  Mute influence implicitly comply.
A wave of splendor and of new delight
  Kindles around the zone beneath thine eye.
Earth hails thee master of material might,
With ever-swelling song and all the charms of sight.

XIV.

When Nature, panting with excess of life,
  Beneath the ripe luxuriance of noon,
Lavished her wealth on the broad landscape rife
  With all the offspring of redundant June,
  Where sighing groves with murmuring brooks commune,
Where meadows wave, or fields of ripening grain,
  Vocal with insect being's drowsy tune,
Where listless herds bestrew the grassy plain
Would Alwyn quaff the scene, till very bliss was pain.

XV.

But when, for many a long and burning day,
    The latest cloud had disappeared on high,
And the white molten sun pursued his way
    Across the surface of a brazen sky,
    Bleaching the earth with unrelenting eye,
When withering pastures crumpled to the tread,
    And brooks exhaled had left their channels dry,
With panting herds he to the shelter fled,
And looked for Nature's death, as if her source were dead.

XVI.

Nor with less awe beheld the Titan war
    Of the returning clouds, so long exiled,
Their angry hosts assembling from afar
    In masses on the low horizon piled,
    Where glorious light, with darkness reconciled,
Rested upon their crests, their armor lined.
    But lo ! they come, swift skirmishers and wild
Sweep o'er the sky, soon with the ranks combined,
And distant thunder rolls up solemnly behind.

XVII.

And heavy drops fall far apart and slow,
    Each on the sand a momentary stain.
The winds leap forth—an ambuscade—and lo !
    The forest writhes and tosses as with pain.
    The dust is swept in clouds along the plain.
Again the thunders issue their command,
    And freely falls the cool refreshing rain,
Copious, but gentle, and with teeming hand
Pours down new stores of life upon the fainting land.

XVIII.

Ye tranquil Summer days, whose breath is balm,
    And soft as rising of the morning dew,
How little wot we that the child-like calm
    Which fills the soul with confidence in you,
    Is but a truce, the balance nice and true
Of such stupendous forces—deadly foes,
    Just waiting with the fatal aim in view—
Ready, when God permits, in strife to close,
Which shall this solid globe dissolve in mortal throes.

XIX.

But evening comes.   And over flood and field
    New changes in succession are displayed,
New outlines on the mountains stand revealed,
    Along the landscape other tints arrayed.
    Reversed the lights and shadows morning made,
And changed the style of all since morning shone.
    Warmer the light and less severe the shade,
While over all steals a soft monotone,
Save where the gorgeous clouds have draped their mon-
        arch's throne.

XX.

Shadows—magicians, at whose lifted wand
    The landscape wakes, and lavish to the sense
Throws life and meaning sparkling o'er the land,
    As kindles up the human countenance
    To inspiration of intelligence—
Whence your strange alchemy, and by what sleight
    Do gladness, beauty, grandeur, wait your glance,
The unsubstantial characters ye write
Along the otherwise unmeaning page of light?

XXI.

The sun has set.   His rays direct withdrawn,
    Gently comes on the scene of day's decline,
The shadows all have blended on the lawn,
    Far sounds the low of home-returning kine,
    Shepherds to the high lair their flocks consign,
The half-reaped field the weary reapers leave,
    Ten thousand insect-notes in choir combine,
The bird sleeps on the spray, and souls conceive
That grateful sense of rest which hails descending eve.

XXII.

The day was full of wonders.   And the night,
    Falling in mystery on the fading view,
Concealed the wonders of the earth from sight
    Only in heaven to open wonders new,
    As with her dusky fingers she withdrew
The veil of light diffused, and from on high
    Poured revelations of creation, through
The opened darkness, on the gazer's eye,
And filled with worlds of light the daily vacant sky.

XXIII.

And as he gazed, and thought of each bright star
    As in itself a world,—for so much lore
Had reached his mountain home,—and tried afar
    Through those stupendous distances to soar,
    His laboring intellect recoiled before
Its own conception of the depths sublime
    Beyond the bounds of earth's encircling shore,
And of the cold dead silence, through all time,
In which those orbs roll on their mighty pantomime.

XXIV.

Yet Alwyn was no vacant looker-on,
    No loitering child of affluence and ease,
Upon his lowly birth no honors shone,
    Nor fortune sought his tender age to please,
    But penury enforced her stern decrees.
Nor did the wise Creator's gracious will
    His childhood from the primal curse release,
But aye with buoyant hope, more gracious still,
From some blest fount within, did all his being fill.

XXV.

Exuberant flow of ever-gushing joy,
    A mystery of the healthful heart and young,
Was his, of all the gifts of the Most High,
    That which most fondly to the lovely clung,
    And common earth with heavenly drapery hung,
Which, like the sun, all other things beheld
    As dyed in hues of its own radiance sprung—
Gift which all other gifts of time excelled,
And grief from his young life effectively repelled.

XXVI.

Well has His work the mighty Maker made
    In mechanism wonderful in man,
And all the parts by many members played
    So harmonized into a common plan,
    So blended soul and body into one,
That all the healthful frame with soul imbued,
    Glorying in existence, its brief span
A full condensed millennium of good,
Bounds with exultant joy—impulsive gratitude.

XXVII.

Hear me, Benignant Author of my days,
    Out of whose bounty all my being came,
In praiseful thanks for the glad life which plays
    In these blue veins, for this material frame,
    Without an organ weak or member lame,
Whose pleasures need nor artifice nor stealth,
    More to my happiness than power or fame,
More than all treasures of redundant wealth,
And for a soul to feel this glorious joy of health.

XXVIII.

And to the woods and hills and running streams,
    And fair, green grassy lawns his heart did burn
With overmastering love. And in the dreams,
    Which Fancy conjured round him, did he turn
    All to account of splendors which would scorn
The actual wealth of kings. And far above
    The utmost bliss that all their power can earn,
Was his at large among the wilds to rove,
Yea, blest as a young bride in her first maiden love.

XXIX.

How wonderful Thy bounty, mighty God,
    So richly to endow the human soul,
Granting it o'er Thy universe abroad
    To rove and gather blessing from the whole,
    Yea, to create, and pleasures to unroll
From that which never was and ne'er shall be,
    And self-sufficing and above control
Of the gross substance, which we hear and see,
Of its own joys and woes to hold the master key.

XXX.

And then, from time to time, a warmer flame
  Eclipsing other feelings of the hour,
Would rush exultant, thrilling through his frame,
  The premonition of a coming power,
  A strange, wild rapture glorying in the dower
Of God within himself, as greater far
  Than all he prized the most in tree, or flower,
In hill, or plain, or sun, or distant star—
Voice of a pent-up gift he cannot yet unbar.

XXXI.

This vague anticipation, whence and why,
  This feeling that I cannot now, but shall,
This consciousness of energies that lie
  Inactive in the spirit's arsenal?
  It came to Alwyn like the secret call
To the boy prophet; but no Eli lay
  Beside him in the temple, who could tell
That it was God who spake. In His own way
Did God Himself instruct His pupil, day by day.

XXXII.

But one wise teacher had the Holiest given,
  In wisdom and in knowledge far above
Her humble rank, rich in the lore of heaven—
  A lovely mother, whose young heart of love
  A few brief years with fondest effort strove
To mold his pliant soul to truth and God,
  Of faith and hope and prayer a garment wove
For his defense on life's unsheltered road.
Then vanished with the call to a more blest abode.

XXXIII.

Nor were companions lacking—leal and true,
  Though unsophisticated peasant hinds;
They loved him well, although they never knew
  His better life, the mystery that binds
  External nature with concordant minds.
And oft they smiled at his impassioned love
  Of such dead things as hills, and streams, and winds,
Nor was himself aware of aught above
Their thinking among whom his thoughts had learned
    to move,

XXXIV.

And in young Norman found, if not a mate
  To all his tastes, at least the complement
Of his affections. Upon neither sat
  The burden of ambition. Well content,
  In humble toil alike their days they spent.
Though far apart their mountain pastures lay,
  And few their meetings; yet with wonder blent,
Did Norman's love upon his neighbor stay—
The dreamy boy who had such weird-like things to say.

XXXV.

And Alwyn loved the lad, whose riper years
  More than himself of common duties knew,
Who humbly practical, as his compeers,
  Saw more than they from Alwyn's point of view,
  And more in him the practical seemed true,
Than in more practical and older men ;
  But most his sweet affections gently drew
Kindred affection to himself again.
Yet ne'er did Alwyn feel so far away as then.

XXXVI.

Yet in his daily tasks among the lone
   And pathless mountains, from the earliest ray
Of golden morning, till the last was gone
   That warmed the evening sky, his Summer day
   Passed far from sight of human life away.
Hills, streams, and rocks, and sighing trees became
   To him society, and in the play
Of living things his heart would often claim
That sense of glad relief man's absence gave to them.

XXXVII.

Where herds intent upon the pasture grazed,
   And nibbling sheep far o'er the mountain spread,
And hares limped by, and listening, stopped, and raised,
   With ever-moving ear, the timid head,
   And the wild deer came nigh with fearless tread,
And birds hung o'er him on the bending spray,
   For hours would he recline beneath the shade,
And yield himself submissive to the sway
Of the unspoken laws those humbler lives obey.

XXXVIII.

Imbibing deep their inarticulate
   Brute sympathies, with sympathy sincere ;
Pondering existence in that strange estate,
   Where, without sense of duty, law, or fear
   Of future ill, the living persevere
In filling the Creator's true intent,
   He felt himself attracted to their sphere,
So humble, yet so free from all complaint,
Without a sin, and yet unconscious of restraint.

XXXIX.

And much he sought the forest dense and old.
  A strange, unhuman charm resided there ;
And in the sombre twilight, damp and cold,
    Which bade the venturous foot of man forbear,
    He found attractions such as dangers wear.
An awful thought that the Almighty God,
    Such as He reigned ere man was made, and ere
Christ was revealed, still had His dread abode
In those old shades, to him was like a wizard's rod.

XL.

Majestic trees, earth's ancient garniture,
  Primeval forests, which so fondly cling
To the wild places, which your life secure
    From the destroying enemy, ye bring
    Conceptions of creation's early Spring,
Ere man's vicegerency had yet begun,
    And when in herb, and stream, and living thing,
In heat, and cold, and cloud, and golden sun,
God solitary reigned, and all His will was done.

XLI.

Not without cause did self-reliant wills,
  Who followed intuition as their guide,
In early times seek God among the hills,
    And 'neath the forest spreading far and wide ;
    Not without cause were altars multiplied
In the dim twilight of your ancient groves,
    Where still a mystery seems to abide,
A presence which the sinful heart reproves,
And where the lonely foot in reverent silence moves.

XLII.

And when I rest beneath your sighing boughs,
   Till in your spirit all my own is clad,
Where passing zephyrs sound like solemn vows,
   Forbidding still, as Nature once forbade,
   Approach of ill, with music soft and glad,
By wild-birds carolled and by streamlets purled,
   I feel as if I too had been half sad
To see the cloudy veil from Eden furled,
And love your dear old remnant of an earlier world.

XLIII.

Upon the outlines, which the mountain's crest
   Boldly against the distant sky defined,
His oft-recurring gaze would fondly rest,
   To variant affections, which combined
   Therewith, all still and passively resigned ;
Held in the meshes of that mystic charm,
   Which in its mastery o'er the human mind,
To soothe or to arouse, depress or warm,
Lives in those soul-subduing boundaries of form.

XLIV.

What tranquil rest reposes in the sweep
   Of curves re-entrant, what joy and pride
Soaring with those which boldly overleap
   The finite, and the easy grace allied
   With undulations which in life preside ;
The dull, depressing angle of the tomb,
   The line direct with truth intensified,
All share in the dominion lines assume
Over the realm of souls to joyfulness or gloom.

XLV.

And ye wild mountains, features of the globe,
   Which else in one dull curvature would lie,
Who weave the varying shadows which enrobe
   Her mighty form with graphic drapery;
   Alone of all her scenes ye lift the eye
And soul to what the better life beseems,—
   The resting-place of clouds where Deity
By ancient men was held to veil His beams,
Patrons of modest vales and ever-laughing streams;

XLVI.

Deep in whose bosom nestles weird Romance,
   In many a solemn glade and dark ravine,
Where day can seldom send a fleeting glance;
   Along whose sides the rolling mists convene,
   Which fairy Fancy peoples with unseen
But potent elves, a baleful multitude;
   While soar your peaks in changeless light serene,
Heaven-scaling Titans ever unsubdued,
Lords of the picturesque in blended fair and rude.

XLVII.

Where were the poetry of earth without
   Your myriad forms? One universal plain,
One curve, forever bending round about
   And downward from the eye, one vast domain
   Of one idea, where the wearied brain
Could find no point of rest; its lord, the soul,
   Sunk in the ever midst, would seek in vain
To rise above the dreary flat, its whole
Conception, or conceive of any loftier goal.

XLVIII.

'Twas not in sermon read from tree or brook,
   Nor rounded sentiment well set and trim ;
'Twas not that objects to his fancy took
   Such conscious forms as Art is pleased to limn,
   Nor in their moral lay their charm to him.
It was enough to live within the reach
   Of things so beautiful, and yield to dim
Delightful feelings which they mutely teach,
Unbroken to the yoke of logic or of speech.

XLIX.

He loved mute Nature, yet had loved less true,
   But that he loved a brighter region more.
What fairy fictions, charming to pursue,
   Forth day by day would fertile Fancy pour.
   And as Imagination learned to soar
Above the world of sense, the eye and ear
   Quickened in their perceptions, and their lore
Accumulated and became more clear,
More beautiful itself and of a nobler sphere—

L.

Incipient impings of immortal mind,
   Unconscious of itself and its estate,
Constrained by native bent to seek and find
   Its greatest bliss wherein its gifts are great,
   And, like its Maker, glory to create.
And books, fair caskets where imprisoned lie
   Spirits familiar, who only wait
The turning of the leaf, by him whose eye
Can break the spell, to wake once more to life and joy,

LI.

Guided to new excursions, opened out
  New regions, where more varied pleasures spring,
And charmed away full many a weakening doubt,
  Till Fancy rose on stronger, lighter wing,
  O'er wider realms a clearer glance to fling,
And in his heart Romance her reign began,—
  Mysterious attractions that will cling
To deeds of other days and life of man,
When deep through mystery wind the inklings of a plan.

LII.

And old and dingy volumes dyed in smoke,
  Drawn from the shelf of many a cottage ben,
Would his prolonged attention oft evoke
  While grazed his flock in silence o'er the glen.
  A chalky pebble was his native pen,
A rock his tablet, and the printed line
  His teacher and his only model, when
He longed in kindred manner to combine
Youth's ardent feelings with its vague and crude design.

LIII.

But when the blasts of Winter swept the hills
  And piled the snow in wreaths adown the vale,
Changed into silent stone the noisy rills,
  Extinguishing the wildbird's joyous tale,
  And filled the air with their own furious wail,
Severer toils befel his feeble years :
  Yet not the less did his glad vision hail
The grandeur which in Nature's wrath appears,
. Her awfulness of gloom, and sadness of her tears.

LIV.

Far from the world of men, alike unknown
   And without knowledge of them or their cares,
And seldom with companions, to his own
   Still thoughts and feelings left, unshaped by theirs,
   And secret of his own, of their affairs
Inquisitive, he early sought to know
   All that the human heart in common shares,
Yet learned it only as a fairy show,
In all the magic light that distance can bestow.

LV.

And in his reading it was Fancy still
   Which marshalled all materials in place,
Led captive with her own fair hands the will,
   Gathered his knowledge into her embrace,
   And robed the whole with her own airy grace.
Much had he learned of knowledge deep and true,
   Much laid to heart which time shall not efface,
Yet had been puzzled sore to set in view
Of other eyes one fact of all the mass he knew.

LVI.

A happy reverence on his spirit lay
   Like moonlight softened through a mellow haze,
Its source unseen, its object far away,
   A simple happiness in prayer and praise,
   A sense of duty drawn from earlier days;
Without a question how God's work proceeds,
   Wherefore He saves from sin, or by what ways,—
A pure blind faith all ignorant of creeds,
Which vaguely trusted One who for the guilty pleads.

LVII.

Learning to wield its earthly instrument
  And grasp the fashion of material things,
The joyful spirit its young vigor lent
    To every task which promised further springs
    Of new sensation. In the bliss that clings
To the first intercourse of earth and soul
    Fully repaid for all the toil it brings,
He garnered stores for future thought's control,
Though unrevealed the end, the means sufficed the whole.

LVIII.

But from the time when sacred Truth began
  To unfold her glories to his wondering eye,
And partially unveil the hidden plan
    Which sends the seasons o'er the changing sky,
    And bids the sons of men their labor ply,
A more ennobling passion ruled his breast.
    No longer mere impressions could supply
Sufficient answer to the spirit's quest,
Which in the light of truth alone could find its rest.

LIX.

One day—a birthday of the mind to him—
  One of those days, in any life but few,
When faint affections and impressions dim,
    By long gestation slowly formed to new
    Conceptions, burst matured upon the view.
On the hill-side he lay, on the smooth green,
    Where oaken boughs their wavering shadows threw,
Far-off the sea, and pastures broad between,
Where spread his fleecy charge in safety o'er the scene.

LX.

His book lay open by his side unread.
  His thoughts were turned upon an inward page,
Whereon the questions and the fears were spread,
    Which ever must, in every land and age,   •
  The anxious thoughts of thoughtful youth engage.
" Whence came this wondrous frame, these hills and streams,
  Yon sea, the winds, the endless war they wage ?
Who made them ? Who sustains them ? Wherefore seems
All earth to love the sun, and quicken in his beams ?

LXI.

" The rivers never weary, even or morn,
  On, on they flow, and ceaseless all night long.
Whence is their life, and wherein are they born ?
    Who sends the clouds ? And what am I among
  Material things so many and so strong ?
Yea, what is life, and whence its force and joy ?
  What gave the ox his strength, the bird his song ?
Who taught the eagle's wing to soar on high,
And knew so well each humbler being to employ ?

LXII.

" And wherefore is there death ? And why the law
  Whereby the young continually supply
The place of those whom age or force withdraw ?
    Who made yon sun ? Who spread that lofty sky ?
    Who carved those vales ? Who built the mountains
      high ?
What are they made of ? How did they begin ?
  Strangest of all, myself, yea, what am I ?
Not long ago I woke, as if within
Eternal night my sleep had co-eternal been.   •

LXIII.

" A long, dark night behind me, and before
 Impenetrable darkness yet to come !
How have I slumbered into life ?   No more.
 •'Tis vain such depths with human line to plumb.
 'Tis vain to question where all earth is dumb.
But this delightful waking, wherein blend
 Both joys and sorrows, and of which the sum
Is ever-growing blessedness, must tend
To some most glorious issue, some exalted end.

LXIV.

" Is it to last forever—to remain
 While God endures, or to return to sleep,
And never, never, never wake again,
 While years on years their endless courses sweep ?
 One thing I know, before me, dark and deep,
An awful, vast eternity is spread,
 And endless life or endless death I reap.
It baffles all my thinking."   Struck with dread,
With wildly throbbing heart he rose and reeling head.

LXV.

What danger in himself could it forebode ?
 A vague, oppressive horror filled his mind.
And as along the mountain side he strode,
 Seeking to toss his questions to the wind,
 Insanity seemed striding on behind.
The emotion passed away ; but from that hour,
 His style of thought was of another kind,
More trenchant it might be, of greater power,
But darkened with a care, whose clouds will ever lower.

LXVI.

In vain the charms of nature lure his eye
  To fill itself and rest in outward things,
In vain enchanting figures floating by
  On Fancy's fairest, most voluptuous wings,
  And ardent Sense her warmest magic flings
Over the living world. A nobler glow
  Kindles his soul; and in its holiest springs
The cause and mystery of life to know
Would he full gladly all the joys of sense forego.

LXVII.

A deeper gulf had opened now between
  Him and his rustic peers; that which divides,
With shadowy bounds, the unseen from the seen.
  What new ambition in his life presides
  Norman will never know. A master guides
The steps of Norman by another way
  As lofty, as mysterious, one which hides
Itself as truly from the common day,
And to be seen demands, not less, a heavenly ray.

LXVIII.

Each had his revelation from on high;
  Yet neither saw the other's aim aright;
Each is entranced by the new realms that lie
  Unveiled before his spiritual sight.
  And yet their joys their spirits disunite.
'Twas not blind faith, but knowledge, Alwyn sought;
  He loved his friend, but held his reason light;
And yet, who knows but higher reason wrought
In him, whose mind possessed the feebler powers of
    thought?

2*

CANTO SECOND.

ANALYSIS.

CANTO SECOND.

I.

To know himself, his being's source to know,
  The speech of outward things to comprehend,
What duties from his true relations flow,
  And whither all the streams of being tend,
  With numerous queries which begin and end
In the vast field such boundaries include,
  Henceforth were points whereon would Alwyn spend
Long, patient thought, aiming as best he could,
To reach by inward light all intellectual good.

II.

At first, 'twas but a vague, though strong desire
  Which had not yet well ascertained its aim—
The half-decided kindling of the fire—
  The reddening glow before it bursts in flame.
  With reverence had he learned each honored name
Among the teachers of the world of old,
  And expectation from their lofty fame,
Looked to their works as treasuries to hold
All wisdom which the mind of mortal can unfold.

(37)

III.

Long labor, and from ruder labors won,
    Unveiled the mysteries of their ancient speech—
Long labor yet, ere half the work was done,
    Conferring treasures sense had failed to reach,
    The unconscious depths of language, into which
He found compressed the heart life of a nation,
    What it had suffered, what it had to teach,
Of its most shrinking secrets the confession,
Hidden by each, and yet by all embodied in expression.

IV.

Wondrous the wealth of living truth that lies
    Deep in a national tongue, as in the earth
Unseen and inconceivable supplies
    Of nourishment for vegetable birth—
    The magnet stones of sorrow and of mirth,
The tillage of the wise.   As earth bestows
    On every plant all that its wants call forth,
So language, ere her noblest writers rose,
Had soared to all their heights and fathomed all their
        woes.

V.

The grand Æolico-Ionian Greek
    Tuned the heroic harp to epic deeds.
The idiom which laboring thinkers speak
    Is ready framed for all that reasoning needs:
    Expression which spontaneously proceeds
From earnest life is deep as life can be;
    And literature must follow where it leads
Through labyrinths of power mysteriously,
And Shakespeare finds in speech a greater still than he.

VI.

The power of Truth—persuasive eloquence—
    The mastery of assemblies—the command
Of nations ; in attack or in defence,
    The weapon most effective for the hand
    Of enemy, most trusty to withstand :
The gentlest touch to soothe the wounded heart,
    The breath of love and friendship the most bland ;
All conquests made in science or in art
Are bound up in the gift which words to men impart.

VII.

And what were God to us without the Word—
    The written Word—the message from on high ?
A power inscrutable, unseen, unheard ;
    And all the hopes that cheer the Christian's eye,
    Making it Christ to live, and gain to die,
Must have remained forever unrevealed.
    A silent God were but an empty sky.
His truth unuttered, and Himself concealed,
What could His works of love, or hope, or pardon yield ?

VIII.

And what were man to man himself without
    The marvellous legacy which words inclose—
The answers to inquiry and to doubt,
    The story of his race, and how it rose,
    The duties which its birth and life impose,
The local mother-tongue, with all its own
    Inheritance of memories, joys and woes,
As every gifted soul, in its own tone
Hears and records the events upon its pathway strewn ?

IX.

And ever lame the effort to translate
   The sentiment of long successive deeds :
The diction which experiences create
   From the profoundest depths of life proceeds.
   Such words are spells, are histories, are creeds;
And he alone hears the reviving strains
   Who feelingly the native symbol reads,
While meditation through deep learning drains
Thoughts of a type, which now in words alone remains.

X.

Thus, day by day, would the enraptured boy
   Dwell on the strains of old Mæonides,
Drinking with new and still increasing joy
   The intoxication of his harmonies,
   Forever varying, like the voiceful seas ;
But to himself as true, as simple, grand.
   What living interest warmed the Epopees !
What graphic art portrayed the Epic land !
While Nature seemed to yield her sceptre to his hand.

XI.

To yield her sceptre, not to lead her slave,
   Nor dictate copy, as to common men.
However great the merit it may have
   Her writing to transcribe with faithful pen,
   A greater gift was his, whose mighty ken
Revealed the Epic world—in the untrue
   To Nature's rule and measure to retain
The charm of Nature, whereby men shall view
All Nature's life, in lives which Nature never knew.

XII.

A glorious world, a region all his own
    Is that evolved in the great minstrel's song,—
The land of Greece—but Greece in mythic dawn,
    While gods enjoyed their paradise among
    Her hills and streams, and when her men were strong
As thrice their number in historic days.
    No earthly science educates his tongue.
The tale he tells, the pictures he portrays,
And all his power of verse, the gift a goddess pays.

XIII.

His heroes till the land, and sweep the seas
    With potent touch, as kings might condescend
To vulgar toil,—and with an Ariel's ease—
    Divine and human in their being blend;
    And in romance their glorious force they spend.
Yet such they are in sentiment and deeds
    As Nature would have made them had she planned
Her work in heroes ; and still thence proceeds
That wherein song's fair realm the realm of fact exceeds.

XIV.

Father of glad Romance, first to suffuse
    The airy fabrics of the brain with truth,
To school in measured art the Aryan muse,
    And out of mythic tales the most uncouth
    And wearisome, with all their depth in sooth,
To weave the web of Epic, and to take
    Captive all ages of admiring youth;
Founder of all that fiction, which can make
Itself such place in art as fact can never shake.

XV.

The Theban eagle, in his sunward flight,
 Alwyn pursued with charmed and eager eye,
Whether through darkening clouds, eluding sight,
 Or flashing out in evening's richest dye,
 Or in eternal Truth's serenest sky
He soared in light, wooing the pure desire
 From earth's renown to nobler things on high.
Then o'er its ashes mourned the Cean fire,
The wreck of Lesbian song, and Sappho's broken lyre.

XVI.

How the heart gladdens in its own bright dream
 Of old Æolian and Doric song!
Bathed in the beauty of that lyric stream,
 Whose waves alone the history prolong,
 All nature smiles; that then were woe and wrong,
That then were irksome toils and cloudy days
 We overlook.   Like future to the young
So to the classic taste the past conveys
Only the poet's world, the magic of his lays.

XVII.

The joyous *Melos* seems to fill the air,
 The buoyant music of a sunny clime,
And Elegy, her sister, not less fair,
 With holy Dithyramb, in her sublime
 Religious ecstacy, blend in the chime
Of choral chants, and festive melodies,
 The voice of Hellas, in her golden prime.
And Ceos, Lesbos, Thebes and Sparta rise
In Fancy's fairest light, to Fancy's dazzled eyes.

XVIII.

To him whose study was the lone hillside,
    Beneath the open firmament, among
The woods, the glens, the land-invading tide,
    There seemed a tie of kindred to belong
    To the great father of dramatic song
With agencies of Nature's mountain reign,
    Whereby the wild, the beautiful, the strong,
Obeyed his wand, in vast ærial train,
As if a Gothic sky had arched the Greek domain.

XIX.

Yet Sophocles more deeply moved his heart
    With pathos of a calmer, steadier glow·—
The model symmetry of tragic art,
    Where line on line, accumulative, slow,
    Fate's dark decrees inevitable grow
Around the path of unsuspecting man
    To all the agony of hopeless woe,
Borne on ·the tide of law, the eternal plan
Of that almighty will, which mortals cannot scan.

XX.

The shrines of old Philosophy he sought,
    And Xenophon's sweet page conned o'er and o'er.
How pure the lucid precepts which it taught,
    And lofty was the object of its lore,
    Fragments of heaven-descended truth it bore.
The being of an all-pervading One,
    Whose mankind are, and whom they should adore,
It taught in lines of light, but light that shone
On the inquiring mind, as distant, cold and lone.

XXI.

But aye, again, again, that charming flow
　　Of sentence calls the lingering student back.
Streams of Socratic dialogue bestow
　　Verdure and health upon their graceful track;
　　And common sense, not here the common hack,
But minister of truth to noblest end,
　　Alike without redundancy or lack,
Does well its message to the heart commend,
Which has no scheme to build, no dogma to defend.

XXII.

And then on Plato's bolder wing he rose
　　To loftier flight, and more extensive view,
Where rays of purer intellect disclose
　　A fairer world, uncircumscribed and new,
　　And strains of eloquence the air imbue,
The faultless labors of the sacred Nine,
　　Whose harmonies the willing soul subdue.
How would he dwell upon the graceful line
In dalliance with truth, and reveries divine,

XXIII.

Now playing with a web of gossamer,
　　To which the breath of Zephyr were a shock,
Now soaring giddily to regions where
　　The glowing rays his waxen pinions mock;
　　Then slowly, surely, as on living rock,
Ascending by the steps of argument;
　　Or stooping some deep secret to unlock
Of thought or passion, while through the extent
Of all his range Delight still followed as he went.

XXIV.

If down from cloudland to the solid earth
　Wise Socrates the muse of Science drew,
Diviner Plato to her place of birth, .
　From earth and clouds alike returned her view.
　He who in God the prime ideas knew,
Must recognize, all dimly though it be,
　In every type of .thought and things, a true
Outgrowth of God ; and thus alone can see
Truth in her changeless forms from all eternity.

XXV.

But over much delusive radiance hung,
　And much was far and indistinctly seen ;
Conjecture to the fairest pictures clung,
　And esoteric phrase would intervene,
　To shade the meaning with its cloudy screen.
Though much of Deity, of men and things
　Those wondrous volumes taught, yet more, I ween,
Was also faintly sketched to guide the wings
Of young inquiry on to more abundant springs.

XXVI.

But more exhausting warfare did he wage
　With obstacles impeding human thought
And its expression, when Stagira's sage
　Before the eye his sterner labors brought,
　His cold analysis, his language caught
From Reason's purest stream, but brief, unkind,
　So closely fitting the conceptions taught,
So unillustrative, the laboring mind
Shrank from the homage due to knowledge thus en-
　shrined.

XXVII.

And yet in that inevitable grasp,
  Which like a higher instinct seized on truth,
Holding it forth in unrelenting clasp,
    As an anatomist the muscle—and in sooth
    With just as little sentiment of ruth
Over its withered life—there was a new,
  Peculiar charm for the inquiring youth,
Which long his deep laborious studies drew,
The tints, indeed, were cold, the drawing still was true.

XXVIII.

But even from truth so chilling, bald and hard,
  He turned away at last in weariness,
The prelude of the philosophic bard
    Luring his spirit with elate address.
    And noble was that symphony, nor less
The grandeur of the whole; but drear the gloom
  Of soul-denying doctrines, which impress
Upon the heart a cold, dark awe of doom,
Of Godless, hopeless fate, and an eternal tomb.

XXIX.

And yet was ever song more weirdly grand,
  With richer beauty in its flowing lines?
Fragments of Eden in a desert land,
    Where desolation with luxuriance joins,
    And Mirage draws her falsely fair designs—
The weight and blackness of the thunder-cloud,
  Edged with the glory of the light which shines
From the deep hidden sun. How lowly bowed
Was heavenly song to theme of dust and death avowed!

XXX.

Brief time, Lucretius, in thy strange domain
   Did the inquiring spirit choose to dwell.
Not all thy harmonies could long retain
   The captive in the magic of their spell,
   While to the soul no tale of life they tell.
Atoms and empty space, and cold and heat,
   With appetence instinctive to compel—
Are these the universe ?   And must we greet
As father of our souls the lifeless bread we eat ?

XXXI.

The theory of Horace might be slim,
   But if " insane," did not afflict him long.
And better far the fickle, weak or dim,
   Than logical consistency among
   Ideas boldly harmonized in wrong,
Compressed, distorted, without sense of ruth,
   Into a system seeming fair and strong,
Fallacious snare of undiscerning youth,
By binding the untrue in common bonds with truth.

XXXII.

A wisdom his emancipate from cant,
   From shiboleths and limits of the schools,
With shams and falsehoods gayly militant,
   The praise of virtue and the scourge of fools,
   Teaching in methods unapproached by rules,
Precise, yet flowing ; negligent, yet terse,
   With genial fancy, which it never cools
The precepts of the sagest to rehearse,
Enrobing truth in fair concinnity of verse.

XXXIII.

Far other was thy glory, Cicero,
   Most fertile genius of the Roman name,
Whose glowing tones of eloquence bestow
   But half thy green inheritance of fame.
   Pure statesman hero, toiling to reclaim .
A sinking country and a vicious age,
   Who lived a life scarce faction dared to blame,
And nobly died to stem the tyrant's rage.
Hail freedom's martyr, hail benign eclectic sage!

XXXIV.

What wisdom in thy pen, from all the past
   Culling the fruits matured, though sparsely sown,
From tomes at which even Study stands aghast,
    And works whose grain of truth had else unknown
    Gone to the grave to which themselves have gone;
From labyrinthine systems all the good
   Weaving into the beauty of thine own,
Enrobing virtue of the manliest mood,
In noblest, sweetest style that e'er reflection wooed.

XXXV.

'Twas almost evidence of truths uproved
   To find the richest thinker of old Rome
Grasping with fondness all that Plato loved.
   For did not souls so nigh of kindred come
   From the same regions of their pristine home?
The Greek to dare the higher flights of mind,
   Till his own subtle speech recoiled therefrom.
But thou, great Tully, wast by Heaven designed
An utterance of thy time, a voice for human kind.

XXXVI.

Within the limits of life's brief career,
  Within the worldly range of Roman view,
Whoe'er proclaimed more cogently and clear
  The purest practice of the good and true,
  Or with a firmer hand exemplars drew
From life, life's joys and duties to display—
  Alike in what from man to man is due,
And what the spirit to itself should pay—
Or lit with holier light its latest earthly day.

XXXVII.

But of the ultimate design in man,
  His origin, his life beyond the grave,
And all that constitutes the Almighty plan
  In virtuous being, or His will to save
  The erring, though thy happy genius gave
The noblest views unaided reason might,
  To nought of all belief unwavering clave.
The *data* lay removed from human sight,
In God's own councils hid, and in primæval night.

XXXVIII.

'Twas thine, great offspring of Hellenic sires,
  From ruder efforts of the earlier time,
From scanty thought and ill-expressed desires,
  From symbol-darkened fragments of sublime
  And God-communicated truth to climb
To heights of science, where the sounds that rise
  Confusedly from below, become a chime
Of perfect harmony, and to the eyes
The far-extended scene blent into beauty lies.

3

XXXIX.

And Plato was thine own.   His lofty mind
   Toiling in truth, as in a diamond mine,
Yet clinging to it only as combined
   With beauty and subservient to design
   By chastest art described with touch divine,
Blest in imagination's richest dower,
   The truest as the grandest type of thine,
Conferred the crown on thy peculiar power,—
Power that must wane, yet last till time's concluding hour.

XL.

Yea, Plato was thine own.   In vain we seek
   Among thy workmen in the world of thought
Another, who so verily the Greek
   On Grecian woof so fair a tissue wrought,
   Making all thine from whencesoever brought;
Not he, who once in Oriental stole,
   In Metapontum and Crotona taught,
Not Socrates, whose comprehensive soul
Embraced all human kind—possession of the whole;

XLI.

Not Aristotle, only Greek by half—
   A half, indeed, of Titan magnitude,
Yet only half—" The wheat without the chaff,"
   Retorts some dialectic, well imbued
   With mysteries of figure, term and mood;
And justly so, were it enough to know,
   And all were done when truth is understood;
Yea, only Greek by half, Parnassus' snow,
Without his Delphic shrine and smiling vales below;

XLII.

Not Zeno, who despised thy love of art,
  And wove a system inhumanely pure,
In which thy darling pleasures had no part,
  Whose fetters for the honors they insure,
  Thy haughty Roman masters might endure,
Believing thus their virtues to recall,
  While monster vices failing still to cure—
But ill-befitting was its gloomy thrall
Thy gayer sons, who sought the beautiful in all ;

XLIII.

Not Epicurus, though a dearer name
  To thy own children, and the Greek supreme
Deemed of Lucretius, who has clothed his fame
  *In colors of a splendor to beseem
  The incarnation of an opium dream ;
Thou lovedst pleasure, but 'twas not to float
  With eyes averted down the giddy stream,
Just blest enough to firmly fail to note
The dangers of the way and frailties of thy boat ;

XLIV.

Nay, not a name among the boasted seven,
  Nor of the mystic Eleatic three,
Can claim that ethnic honor, proudly given
  By grateful souls of thinking men in thee,
  To him the sage of the Academy,
Whose plastic spirit, once for all defined
  In shape for all succeeding time to see,
That fair philosophy which Grecian mind,
Though striving oft in vain, still natively designed.

XLV.

Far other was the work of lordly Rome.
Not hers to watch and wait the dawning thought,
Till troops of new and dazzling fancies come
    From the deep bosom of preceding nought,
    Or that dark chaos whence unseen are brought
The atoms of conception. Not in her
    Was it that innate Beauty ever sought
For self-development, or dared to stir
Those springs of pure delight which new-born thoughts
    confer.

XLVI.

Far other work—to conquer and to rule,
    To stamp her impress on each neighboring land.
For this she culled from every Grecian school
    Wisdom matured to guide her forceful hand,
    And rifled every mystery of command,
To build a structure of enduring laws,
    And government which should forever stand,
To force obedience and to win applause
On the foundation laid of Nature's deepest cause.

XLVII.

Let others search for truth, and prove it true,
    Her mighty arm was destined well to wield
The tempered weapon, while its edge was new,
    In actual combat on the living field ;
    Till even they by whom it was revealed,
Rejoiced submissive in that sovereign reign,
    Which to their doctrines wider range could yield,
Beholding the results of studious pain
Diffused by Roman hands through all her vast domain.

XLVIII.

Greek to discover,—Roman to diffuse,—
　To bear the seeds of knowledge all abroad,
The brave protector of the Orient muse
　Who opened up her Occidental road,
　Enlarged the ancient bounds of her abode,
Till from the sands of Nubia to the Rhine,
　And from the Tigris to the Atlantic flood
Learning and Rome beheld their arts combine
To soothe discordant wills and barbarous lives refine.

XLIX.

" And who with most effect," did Alwyn ask,
　" Among the cohorts of Rome's mighty men,
In execution of this mental task,
　Wielded the lucid philosophic pen,
　Pursuing the far flight of Grecian ken
While winning pupils of the old and young ?"
　Who but the same upon whose diction, when
Flowing in magic from his living tongue,
The listening thousands long in silent rapture hung ?

L.

Then was it not of appetence divine—
　The inly felt commission from on high—
Which led great Tully to the greater shrine
　Of Academic wisdom, to supply
　Its practical defects from stores that lie
Scattered among the schools of every creed ?
　Yea, such the guidance of the Eternal eye,
That all their toils to one result might lead,
And nations should confess the spirit's worth and need.

LI.

Yet master, as he was of all the range
  Of his own art and of his native tongue
Commanded, like a wizard, every change,
    The grave, the gay, the gentle, and the strong,
    And distant ages still his praise prolong;
Was there not one a truer type of Rome,
    In all her majesty of right and wrong,
Her law abroad and laxity at home,
Her lordly power to rule, as force to overcome?

LII.

Not suddenly, but grandly, line by line,
  Self-drawn did Cæsar rise before his ken,
Clothed with the mastery of a gift divine,
    By personal fascination to enchain,
    To wield the might of armies, or the pen,
Or gather legislation in his hands,
    Greatest of Romans, if not first of men,
Whose name still as the name of empire stands,
And still the living as the ancient world commands.

LIII.

Two masters, born in times not far apart,
  Have to the world its highest culture lent,
One planted his commission in the heart,
    The other in the forms of government.
    And now, almost two thousand years are spent,
And still those mighty masters rule the same,
    The world's best order follows their intent
And Cæsar still divides with Christ the claim,
And over against Christ's is ever Cæsar's name.

LIV.

Yet Cæsar's power is waning, and must wane,
  And Christ's the narrower once, expands meanwhile,
And will expand, though Cæsar's must remain
  Till Christ has vanquished violence and guile.
  One or the other, in his several style,
Must rule where men are upright or refined.
  With force or love our lives we reconcile.
Law or the gospel. The best human kind
Are Cæsar's until Christ is in their hearts enshrined.

CANTO THIRD.

ANALYSIS.

Canto III.—Alwyn seeks new sources of instruction—Removes to the city—Connection with journalism—Dissatisfied with the intellectual results—The university—Definite aims for proper self-culture—Seeks facilities for studying the modern literature of Continental Europe—Rouen—French literature—German —Italy—View of Tivoli—Traces of human antiquity—Their effect upon the mind—Hebrew and Oriental literature— English literature.

CANTO THIRD.

I.

But Alwyn, while his zeal of learning sped
    From source to source, perceived approaching lack,
When, at the pastor's shelves no longer fed,
    He must submit to turn its ardor back,
    And pace henceforward in the common track.
The buoyant heart which had led on so far,
    Bounded once more into the new attack
On difficulty, in this joyous war,
Nor felt in " poverty unconquerable bar. "

II.

" My native mountains, whose grey summits write
    Their daring outlines on the azure sky,
I love the manly lessons ye indite,
    The self-reliance and the purpose high,
    The liberty of thought which ye supply.
But 'tis of God, not man ye have to teach,
    And I would also learn of man, and try
Paths of instruction, which I cannot reach
Among your wilds, where all is strange to human speech.

(59)

III.

"I love it not, the crowded, murky town,
　　Yet there are treasures, which I fain would seize ;
And Learning there extends her laurel crown—
　　Though crowns I reck not, nor her bald degrees—
　　Baubles designed the shallow mind to please.
But much I long to sit at Learning's feet,
　　And drink her drafts of knowledge to the lees.
For this farewell each wild and calm retreat,
And welcome smoke and dust, the foul and noisy street.

IV.

"In thee, my own fair land of hill and plain,
　　Of fertile vales and shining peaks of snow,
I fain would find that intellectual gain.
　　If not, then elsewhere must my footsteps go,
　　For know I must all God will have me know.
To part with thee will cost me many a sigh,
　　But through my being burns a ceaseless glow,
Which is my life, and if it dies, I die,
And if unfed it lives, I burn eternally.

V.

"The daily journal is the people's king.
　　His ministers are princes.　Their control,
Pervasive as the agencies of Spring,
　　And generative as they, as broad and full,
　　Insinuates itself into the soul,
And works its purpose by creating will,
　　And through the individual wields the whole.
In his vast court the lowliest place I'd fill,
Only to breathe that air of knowledge, good and ill."

VI.

An humble choice; but not an humble aim.
    Where every athlete strips him for the race,
Talent asserts successfully her claim,
    And bounds to higher and to higher place,
    'Twixt high and low the distance to efface,
And sweep the adventitious out of view.
    So Alwyn rose—and rose in public grace,
Into the columns of the journal threw
His own deep fervor, and his thinking bold and new.

VII.

Scanty, at first, his skill of men, I ween,
    But quick his tact in everything that lay
Before him, and of penetration keen,
    He seized upon the topics of the day,
    And dashed them off, in an impassioned way.
While young assurance passed for conscious might,
    And needed only diction to array
The news that could be gleaned by ear or sight,
The public read and praised with wonder and delight.

VIII.

Not that in truth or substance there was aught
    In article of his elsewhere unknown;
Nothing was there of reach or depth of thought,
    The buoyancy of joyous life alone
    Breathed through his style its warm and gladsome
Like the aroma of a precious wine,   [tone,
    Ineffable in all that was its own,
It filled the reader's heart with a benign
Delight, as if he too possessed the gift divine.

IX.

Successful toil increase of toil incurred,
    Duties fulfilled to higher duties led,
Until Necessity full often spurred
    To effort which no gushing impulse fed,
    A task not of the heart, but aching head.
The journal, which at first appeared a friend,
    A messenger of what was to be said,
Became a monster despot, in the end,
Whose daily life by lives of men must be maintained.

X.

Wearisome days have mounted up to years,
    And where the lore wherein he hoped to bask ?
The toil remains, but not the joy that cheers,
    When youthful ardor kindles every task ;
    Gold has flowed in, for which he did not ask,
Knowledge of things which gave him no concern,
    Mysteries of life he cared not to unmask ;
But all that knowledge he had hoped to earn
Seemed further now away and harder now to learn.

XI.

Before the world a teacher and a guide
    Of national opinion, to advise
How men should think, and how they should provide
    For public wants the adequate supplies,
    He stands most painfully in his own eyes
Unfurnished with a knowledge of the laws
    On which a people worthily relies,
And all unfit to labor in a cause
Which from profoundest truth its only safety draws.

XII.

Disgusted with himself the more he felt
  The grandeur of his work and its demands,
The uneasy spirit obstinately dwelt
  Upon itself as wrong.   The guilty bands—
Guilty to him—he severed from his hands.
How much he yet must know of living truth,
  Of present times, their letters and their lands.
This work in doubt and crudities uncouth
Could but mislead the mass and squander fleeting youth.

XIII.

A true and earnest modesty, in league
  With pride, from aught but perfect work restrained.
Ah, then, amid reaction and fatigue,
  When effort had the vital forces drained,
  And in his heart humiliation reigned,
The lowlier aims of Norman did not seem
  Of such a nature as to be disdained.
At least pretence did not outrun esteem,
And promise was not more than practice could redeem.

XIV.

And was not Norman happy in his way,
  Beloved by one whose warm affections shed
The purest light of life on every day,
  Rejoicing in the work which earned his bread,
  And with no higher cravings to be fed,
Save those of simple faith, by which he held
  A life in Christ, his spiritual head.
Alwyn admired, and yet his heart rebelled—
By one strong ruling force all other force compelled.

XV.

" The holiest, as the highest act of man
    Is to believe the truth, and well to know
  Its circulation in the eternal plan
    Of being.   But in the inscrutably slow
    And ponderous round by which the ages go,
I would explore likewise the written Word ;
    If haply there some Logarithmic law
Solution of the complex all afford.
For me let this be love and friendship's sweet accord."

XVI.

Within a lovely lawn of fair extent,
    And through whose length a slumbrous river slept,
Rose Halls where youth, on lofty themes intent,
    It was presumed perpetual vigils kept.
    No noisy fleets of trade that river swept ;
No cares distracting ventured to invade
    The cloistered walks where Meditation stept.
But aye the hush of Sabbath stillness paid
Reverence to patient thought, which waiting loves the
       shade.

XVII.

Light galleys floated softly without sound
    Between the banks of smoothly-shaven grass,
And bore, as if within enchanted ground,
    Thinkers whose only work in life it was
    To harness thoughts, instructed as they pass,
Into the service of the good and true ;
    Readers who gather wisdom as a glass
Gathers the burning rays by steady view.
'Twas what Alwyn had dreamed, but more than Fancy
       drew.

XVIII.

Upon an ancient gate-way dark and low
    He read the word " Humility," and said,
" Most fit should I beneath that portal go,
    As by humiliation hither led."
    And soon through that " Of Labor " also sped,
He sought his own consent, with vain delay,
    To pass the gate " Of Honor," ill bestead
With ignorance which filled him with dismay,
Till from his mind all thought of honor passed away.

XIX.

Of higher import far to him the care,
    Had he acquired what manhood's duties crave,
The knowledge and the wisdom which prepare
    To rightly use the gifts the Master gave ?
    Harvests of ripened learning round him wave ;
Yet half it seems to him like doubling sound
    Within a vast reverberating cave.
From the dark walls a thousand voices bound ;
And yet in all the tones of cnly one are found.

XX.

The College has its hero, whose great fame
    Her younger sons like breath of life inhale.
And if the greater number miss the aim,
    And not as his their blanching toils avail,
    They drink, at least, the potion that makes pale.
The hero may be glorious in his way,
    A Newton, or a Porson, yet entail,
By force of an involuntary sway,
A bondage which shall long the step of Truth delay.

XXI.

" Where knowledge is an instrument designed
    To act on human life as formative—
Though oft with bias obstinate and blind—
    To plastic youth a purposed bent to give,
    'Tis wisely urged by force competitive.
But why should I, not of the brotherhood,
    Nor wishing ever by such skill to live,
Subject myself to methods thus pursued,
And sell my birthright so in every higher good ?

XXII.

" Beyond all estimate the truth here stored,
    Beyond all praise the toiling minds, who earn
Its honors and who coin the massive hoard.
    But what the College knows the youth must learn ;
    Not how to estimate or to discern
Things independently.   Correct and slow,
    Bordered by banks of stone, direct and stern
As a canal, from centuries ago,
Its stream of thought flows on, as ever taught to flow.

XXIII.

" On the great map of human life the lines
    Of latitude and longitude of powers
May cover all ; but no such law assigns
    Identity to trees and fruits and flowers,
    All gifted with their own respective dowers.
One sun to all his radiance must impart,
    To all alike the falling of soft showers ;
And yet each kind grows by a different art.
So lives its proper gift in every human heart.

XXIV.

" That germ of higher life to scrutinize,
Its proper culture and its aims secure,
Distinct from what philosophers comprise
In laws of human nature, must insure
The highest good, and longest to endure.
For thus to follow nature is not sin.
The special gift is in itself most pure.
Sin is the common lot. Deeper within
The temple lies the law where virtue must begin.

XXV.

" Rouen stands queenly by the winding Seine,
And gathers gain, who once commanded praise,
All heedless of her mediæval reign,
The warlike grandeur of her early days,
When knights, the themes of mighty minstrels' lays,
Trod her resounding streets, her stately halls.
Enough that England's gold her toil repays ;
The pride that native once within her walls
Reigned England's Conqueror, no busy head recalls.

XXVI.

" And wherefore should she alway dream of eld,—
Of rule which never more she can command ?
Yea, let the empty by-gone be dispelled.
But why should here that virgin statue stand
With its condemning memories to brand
Thy reputation with unmanly crime ?
Then fell thy arm—the weapon from thy hand.
Here I arrest my steps. For here things chime
In with my mood for old, merging in present time."

XXVII.

Thus Alwyn flees afar—yea, far from all
   Who ever knew him or his native speech.
Not that he hates mankind, but that the call,
   Which ever seems within him to beseech,
   Invites to ends no social labors reach.
" In this old capital of Normandie
   I'll seek again what lonely toil can teach.
The something above sense God grant to me
To rightly apprehend, the good in life to see."

XXVIII.

And now with clearer purpose to explore
   The mines of thought, his ardent steps advance
From classic treasures of long garnered store,
   To thy still growing fields, illustrious France.
   Thy formal verse he measured with a glance,
Which not the pure Racine could long delay ;
   But O, what rapture did his soul entrance
When o'er thy charming prose he held his way,
By the quiet mystic led, the Mentor of Cambray,

XXIX.

By lofty Massillon, from whence the view
   Embraced two brother streams, far flowing on,
The broad and full Bosuet, and Bourdaloue
   Direct and rapid as the Alpine Rhone ;
   Rouseau, a fairy hill, but sad and lone ;
Pascal, a lake, pure mirror of the sky,
   Cold Rochefoucauld in glittering crystals shone ;.
Montesquieu, a vineyard rich and high ;
A garden Saint Pierre of many a lovely dye.

XXX.

And La Bruyere, and Vauvenargues, Duclos,
  Were cultured farms and fields of waving grain,
And as a forest tossing to and fro
    In changing winds along a mountain chain,
    The numerous heroes of thy later reign;
While many a castle, well defended, crowned
    The rocky steeps, and awed the distant plain,
Wherein philosophy had early found
Congenial home, and still retained her vantage ground.

XXXI.

And when his journey closed, the lingering strain
  Which longest held possession of his ear,
Came from the pulpit.   In her noblest reign,
    The lettered muse of France, doomed to appear
    Too oft the friend of error, chose to rear,
As if all future censure to disarm,
    Her fairest structures polished and severe,
Pure as Athena's temple, of the warm
Gospel of Christ, in lines forevermore to charm.

XXXII.

Grateful we yield what admiration owes
  To controversial fervor in Bosuet,
To solemn hopes, and Christian repose
    In Flechier; or higher tribute pay
    To Art, where Nature chooses to obey
The wand of Massillon; and for the true
    Native and incommunicable sway,
The gift which Art, subserving, never knew,
Nature will fondly claim, with heart-throbs, Bourdaloue.

XXXIII.

And then, with ardent, long expectant toil,
    He climbed to other language heights, and viewed
The scene of Teuton warfare and turmoil,
    Where scholars, critics, sophists urged the feud,
    With erudition vast, and deep imbued
With theories the outer public's scorn,
    In dreary tomes, laborious, shapeless, crude,
And yet from out that chaos saw, like morn,
A nation's literature in glad effulgence born—

XXXIV.

A literature self-conscious from its birth,
    Built up by critic skill, to order made,
By rule prescribed, and yet of native worth,
    Racy and fresh in living truth arrayed,
    Where wisely Art has come to Learning's aid,
And from the mystic depths of German mind
    Called up a new Parnassus, and essayed
New forms, in which her products are defined,
And of the German heart the warmth and worth en-
       shrined.

XXXV.

But onward still enthusiasm led,
    Kindling by motion to a fiercer glow ;
Language itself assumed a charm that fed
    The fervor of pursuit.   And still to know
    Another and another, and to throw
Open another gate of thought became
    A triumph and a joy, as if a foe
Were vanquished.   And again to seek the same
Exultant sense of power was fuel to the flame.

XXXVI.

Those two fair daughters of a Roman mother,
   Who still her old inheritance retain,
Of majesty, the one, and grace, the other,
   Beneath the skies of Italy and Spain,
   Spread to his eye the wealth of their domain,
Rich in the fruits of music and of song:
   One in the utmost life from Art can gain ;
The other, artless truth and passion strong,
And wild adventure drawn from warfare practiced long.

XXXVII.

And thou, O Italy, though for the eye
   A thousand charms thy varied land combines,
Thy ever-neighboring sea, and cloudless sky,
   Thy fertile plains, traversed by graceful lines
   Of elms that bend to wed the climbing vines,
Thy mountain ranges, and thy rushing streams,
   Hast yet a magic which no form confines,
But breathing round one in delightful dreams,
More to the glowing heart than all the landscape seems.

XXXVIII.

Above fair Tivoli the mountains rise
   Shaggy and wild, and wavy lands below
Extend afar to the engirdling skies ;
   While from her throne of rocks, like sheet of snow,
   Her torrent river plunges, in its flow
Piercing the opposing ledge, and on its breath
   Wearing, in joyous light, the Iris bow,
As into Stygian darkness, far beneath
The giddy, reckless wave descends, like life to death.

XXXIX.

Her olive groves and green declivities,
    Her sunny fields which feed the clustering vine,
Grottoes and glades, to which the herdsman flees,
    And where his flocks at sultry noon recline,
    Are threads in feeling's web that sweetly twine ;
And yet the eye will turn from all to rest
    With fonder love upon yon Sibyl's shrine ;
Nor in its fair proportions find the best.
A dearer gift is there—Antiquity's bequest—

XL.

The gift of centuries, memory of a race
    Whose deeds are lessons, and whom to admire
Is half the way to greatness.   Thus we trace
    The lines which Ruin's old domains inspire :
    Here Horace mused, here Tully's soul of fire
Fed on new beauties, Cæsar's march delayed,
    And gay Catullus tuned his graceful lyre ;
Sallust his graphic pictures here portrayed,
And lonely musing, here the sad Tibullus strayed.

XLI.

Then vague, but vast and glowing visions rise
    Of manful Rome, invincible and free,
And of a gorgeous empire fierce, yet wise
    To hold of wisest men the sovereignty,
    And mold mankind for what they were to be ;
Visions of classic art and vandal wrong,
    And of a wintry intervening sea—
Ages of discord, whence harmonious sprung
    The elements of art, when art again was young.

XLII.

Earth holds a concord with the heart of man,
  Her forms and hues and voices manifold,
All find their own dominion there and fan
    Their kindred feelings.   And the reign they hold
    Is of a wealth unmeasured and untold.
And yet one footprint of a by-gone age,
  One page of human history unrolled,
Is more to rouse emotion, or assuage,
Than all the assembled charms of Nature's heritage.

XLIII.

And then the native language of that book,
  Now taught to speak in every human tongue,
Upon whose lessons he had learned to look
    As from the councils of the Highest sprung,
    Around his heart its inspiration flung,
That speech before whose venerable eld
    Rome was of yesterday and Greece was young,
And yet the force within whose bosom held,
Is still unmarred by time, its mastery undispelled.

XLIV.

The rosy light, which half-reveals, half-veils
  The graceful luxury of orient climes,
That magic of romance, which even tales
    Of wild untruth, and arbitrary crimes
    Into the heaven of Poetry sublimes,
Allured his toils, where novel regions teem
    With thoughts unfixed by places, or by times,
Which floating in a mist of fancy seem
Like forms of cloudland born, and wilful as a dream.

4

XLV.

And thus from land to land, day after day,
  Enthusiasm rushed with joyous bound.
Not that his knowledge yet had seen the way
  To that strange mystery, most to astound,
  That all the loftiest, truest, most profound
Philosophy that ever man conceived
  Is with the language which he speaks inwound,
That all his mind or prowess has achieved,
All he has loved, or hated, questioned or believed,

XLVI.

All he has been, as light upon the page
  By photographic skill prepared, records
Itself in living speech from age to age :
  Alwyn ransacked the gallery of words
  For the more finite pictures it affords
Of fair conceptions drawn by greatest men.
  And sooner than expected were those lords
Of languages subjected to his ken.
Few from all time the master-pieces of the pen.

XLVII.

Meanwhile had Springs and Autumns come and fled,
  And youth had been by riper age replaced,
His native literature so long unread,
  Which largely earlier studies had embraced,
  Was less from memory than esteem effaced.
But when he bade a truce to that long war
  In foreign fields, and former walks retraced,
It was with thoughts such as the traveler's are
When home again he greets, returning from afar.

XLVIII.

" All hail, again, my native English tongue,
    Thou comest on my ear so richly fraught
With melodies from life's deep fountains sprung,
    And harmonies of feeling and of thought,
    I seem to hear the voice of her who taught
My infant lips to shape themselves to thee,
    Of those who in youth's giddy passions wrought
The work of love, of hate, of grief, of glee,
Of beauty's holy rest, or rapt solemnity.

XLIX.

Each word and accent has a tale to tell,
    Like early friends met under foreign skies,
And as I yield me passive to thy spell,
    Upon imagination's canvas rise
    Their forms—the good, the beautiful, the wise—
Who taught the aspiring soul its noblest aim,
    Nor absent his who labored to devise
Temptation to its ruin, and whose name
Still kindles up disgust, or anger's keener flame.

L.

Nor does my spirit its own past career
    Alone from thy resources thus repair,
The thoughts of millions fill thine atmosphere,
    As warm and genial sunlight fills the air—
    Thine atmosphere in which the odors rare
Are poetry, and science is the gale,
    And he who therein lives, though it may bear
At times miasma's transitory bale,
Knowledge and beauty must, as daily breath, inhale.

LI.

Thou humblest thyself to every care,
  The lowliest task to human labor known.
And in assuaging revelation where
    Languish the poor, disease's victims groan,
    Or conscience-stricken wretches would atone
For bitter guilt by self-condemning tale,
  Hast thou the gates of utterance open thrown.
And where thy deep heart-searching meanings fail,
Where fail they ever must, what other can avail?

LII.

But when a Hamlet's or Othello's woe
  The pangs sublime of pandemonian king,
Immortal triumph o'er immortal foe,
    Or the glad theme which ransomed spirits sing,
    Demand the service of a bolder string,
As little do thy harmonies refuse.
    Nay, rising buoyant as an angel's wing,
Where thy high argument its path pursues,
Thou soarest beyond the flight of Greek or Roman muse.

LIII.

What words like thine supply the fluent tongue
  With instruments of winning eloquence,
Which, scattering to the winds the arts of wrong,
    And sifting equally from the pretense
    Of anarch and of despot honest sense,
Can charm into conviction, and inspire
    That pure delight words can alone dispense,
When to high meaning chimes their lofty choir,
And Truth from Beauty draws new cogency and fire.

LIV.

Such was the sceptre by thy Wilberforce,
  Thy Burke, thy Murray, and thy Canning swayed,
Till tyrants, yielding, smiled on Freedom's course,
  And legal rapine in his rage was stayed.
And yet more glorious thy achievements made
In nations kindled to the heavenly call
  By Whitefield's seraph tongue, and faith arrayed
In science and in eloquence, from all
The intellectual wealth of Chalmers and of Hall.

LV.

And yet they say there's harshness in thy tone.—
  It may beseem the vain who boast their lore
In other tongues, though smatterers in their own,
  To vaunt the value of their foreign store,
  And sneer at the capacious chords which pour
Alike the solemn organ notes that swell
  The song of Paradise, the Lays of Moore,
The Doric strains of Burns, and those that dwell
With Cowper, Coleridge, Scott, and Wordsworth's Druid
    shell,

LVI.

Which from the warblings of unhappy Clare,
  And the sweet minor of a Tannahill,
To fiercest wailings of sublime despair,
  Which to the sweeping touch of Byron thrill
  The bosom which they subjugate and fill
With all a Titan's suffering, command
  The diapason of the heart and will ;
But elsewhere seeketh not the master's hand
For keys to speak the true, the lovely, or the grand.

LVII.

Interpreter of free and ardent souls,
  Wise in thy strength, unshackled by the fear
Of censorship, whose living thunder rolls
    Majestically truthful and severe,
    The foes of liberty to blast and sear—
The flaming sword of Chatham, Fox, and Brougham,
  Nor less of him whose kindling words could rear
The standard of the free, dispel their gloom,
Could bid a nation live and men their rights assume.

LVIII.

Full true, thou hast thy discords, sharp and loud
  (And so hath Heaven), against the hour of need.
On whomsoever bursts thy thunder-cloud
    Has found thy wrath no opera chant indeed,
    Nor set to measures of the " melting reed."
For every passion of the human breast,
  All trains of thought, however they proceed,
And every curious topic of inquest,
Thou hast a fitting garb and armor of the best.

LIX.

Grant me to know the treasures of thy reign,
  To wield at will the wealth which they afford,
For every whim, conviction, joy, and pain,
    Promptly to grasp thy well-befitting word ;
    With thee to launch into the far explored
Yet boundless regions of the human soul,
  I shall not envy Polyglotts their hoard,
Though fair the dormant pile.   The full control
Of current life like thine transcends the boasted whole

CANTO FOURTH.

ANALYSIS.

CANTO IV.—Philosophy, its elevated place in human knowledge—Founders of true philosophy, the world's indebtedness to them—Early feelings after truth—Ambitious speculation a feature of crude philosophy—The Ionian school, the Eleatic, Italic—Socrates—Necessity of method—Its various aims—Why the knowledge of truth is of vital importance towards making the best of human nature—Man him*self* the central point of all true philosophy—The *self* essentially the unseen element of man's being—A present *self* in relation to all other human selves—Its relations to God—Views of God, His duration—Bewildering questions—A mathematical philosophy—The transcendental—The tempest of controversy—A better philosophy—The lesson of Socrates to be forever remembered—Faith in nature—Gains from study of philosophy.

CANTO FOURTH.

I.

"Divine Philosophy, to thee I bow,
  And pay the reverence to thy labors due,
Co-agent of the written Word.   For thou
  Art revelation from Jehovah too,
  Made to the patient student of the true.
As that unfolds the plans of heavenly grace
  The great Creator's image to renew,
So led by thee, the spirit learns to trace
The way where wisdom leads our widely erring race.

II.

Though second to the Word, yea humbler far
  Than inspiration of the poet seer,
And silent often where enquiries are
  Of highest import, and the hopes most dear,
  Transcending all the rest vouchsafed us here.
As, like the clouds of fertilizing rain,
  Thy fruits spring where thou ceasest to appear,
So slanderers scout thee, while they reap the gain
Which at thy bounteous hand alone they can obtain.

4*   (81)

III.

How poor the good this mortal life could bring
   From all its dormant stores, without thy aid?
And feeble were the flight of fancy's wing,
   If not upon thy steady pinion stayed.
   So deep, so widely do thy works pervade
The social frame, that they who scarcely know
   The meaning of thy name, and never made
Confession of the mental debt they owe,
Live by thy truths proclaimed thousands of years ago.

IV.

What gave their glory to the great of old?
   What made the Attic Greek and Roman great?
Were not the Spartan and the Samnite bold
   In equal warfare?   Whence their humbler fate?
   Philosophy debarred their ruder state,
They failed in purpose large, digested, clear,
   In judgment, when to hasten, when to wait,
Or to subdue to any bond save fear,
All that their valiant hosts vanquished with sword and
     spear

V.

Shortsighted counsels lost; and prosperous war
   Was only glorious bloodshed, and conferred
No other gain than rebel subjects are.
   Conquests were but a gangrene—only stirred
   A deadlier fire of vengeance, and deterred
The voluntary homage of the free.
   Far otherwise the nobler states, which heard
And reverenced the counsels given by thee,
Built up a rule of which the world is proud to be.

VI.

Each conquest was a fortress.   The subdued
    By force of arms, soon gloried in the fame
Of masters who bestowed substantial good,
    While lending all the splendor of their name.
    And allies with a free submission came,
A barbarous independence well to pay
    For civil form and life, until the same
Spirit pervaded all beneath their sway,
And back upon its source came each reflected ray.

VII.

And where had been the boast of later times
    But for the legacy of old bequeathed,—
The freedom of these occidental climes,
    Arts of the south, which when the sword is sheathed,
    Still blossom 'neath the genial fragrance breathed
From ancient genius; or the learnéd brow
    Still with the laurel of Apollo wreathed,
The legal codes to which the nations bow,
And debts of social forms, which never debts avow?

VIII.

And what had been their legacy to leave,
    But for their students of the true and fair?
Such as the tribes of Africa receive
    From ancient times had fallen to our share.
    Sweep from the world all that the Muses bare,
All that the sage, and poet-sage proclaimed,
    The Hebrew schools, the songs that echoed there,
Those holiest words by human language framed,—
The moral lays which first the Grecian mind enflamed,

IX.

The labors, with their aye perennial fruit,
    Of the profoundly, rightly thinking few,
Of Solon, of Pythagoras—the root
    Whence many a stem of truth luxuriant grew,
    Of wisest, patient Socrates, the true
Prometheus of our race, without his woes,
    And of the minds his lucid genius drew,
Of Xenophon, of Plato, and of those
In Elis and Cyrene, and Megara who rose,

X.

Of Aristotle, of Carneades,
    Of Zeno, of Panætius, Cicero,
Of Paul, who taught the Christian mind to seize
    That dialectic power the schools bestow,
    The sons of Greek and Roman song, who owe
Their master-spell to truth and hope and trust,
    Which only from Philosophy can flow,
With all their offspring, and this being must
Sink to the humblest joys of animated dust.

XI.

Yet, in thy realms of science many a way
    Of devious but attractive error lies.
Thousands have found thy fields only to stray,
    And ever seek, with misdirected eyes,
    Not Truth, but deadly Falsehood in disguise.
And there are questions of the loftiest kind,
    To which thy voice can render scant replies.
Thy lights are ever matched by shades behind,
And he who loves thee must not to thy faults be blind.

XII. .

In that which Alwyn most had yearned to know,
He still remained untaught. The skeptic's pen
Had labored much, not fruitlessly, to show
  That ignorance must ever baulk the ken,
  As time the being of the sons of men,
That life is but a dream, from which we ne'er
  Awake, but ever, ever dream in vain,
Through mingled phantasms of joy and care,
Till back to nothingness our weary way we fare.

XIII.

And in the ancient lessons which he chose,
  As primary, to open up his way,
Questions of darkest mystery arose,
  And systems which pretended to display
  Alike the growth of being and decay
And birth, where man finds nothing to adore,
  Nothing to trust in, follow or obey.
Philosophy's young wings the wildest soar
Through realms inscrutable, with most ambitious lore.

XIV.

Ionian science boasted to declare
  How things arose, and out of what they grew—
Of holiest water, fire, earth or air,
  As each Sophistés from his fancy drew.
  Italic wisdom held the guiding clew
To the bewildering labyrinth of things
  In law, which harmonizing old and new,
Out of confusion fairest order brings,
Till in the joy of beauty, the glad cosmos rings.

XV.

The Eleatic labored to enlist
    The toil of thought in being sole and pure—
·The energy in which all things consist,
    Of which they are, and by which they endure,
    Which well to know is wholly to secure
The knowledge of the all. Nor wiser they,
    In their own wisdom no less vainly sure,
Who built the worlds by their well ordered play
Of Atoms, leaving man to his own sovereign sway.

XVI.

"Hope not," the ancient sage Ephesian taught,
    "For aught beyond this ever-rolling sphere.
Hopes of the perfect are but waste of thought,
    And all we know must dwell forever here.
    'Tis not progression which pervades the year,
But revolution. And as cycles roll,
    The past must in the present reappear;
By whom directed, to what distant goal,
'Tis vain to ask. A part embraces not the whole."

XVII.

Of Cyrenaics humbler the design
    For human life, to set its pleasures free.
"The proudest temple is an empty shrine,
    Elysium but the tale of Poesy,
    For who has looked into Eternity,
Or who has come from Pluto's gloomy hall,
    Or to discover the divine decree
Has overleaped Heaven's adamantine wall?
Why doubt, or fear, or hope? Enjoy, and thou hast all."

XVIII.

In vain the laboring spirit seeks repose
  Upon the artifice of such replies.
Nor, though a purer life his creed bestows,
  Much less in vain the Cynic's hope to rise
  To all perfection of the good and wise
Through subjugation of the outer sense.
  'Tis not enough thus to philosophize,
However craftily, if one commence
With fiction, for which all his craft fails of defence.

XIX.

'Twere well to know of what all things were made;
  'Twere well into the primal cause to see,
To listen to the choral music played
  By chiming spheres in heavenly harmony,
  Were they within our reach, or could they be
Attained by bold conjecture. But if no
  Amount of striving sets their secret free,
Were it not better to come down below,
And, with an humbler aim, make certain as we go?

XX.

And there are higher interests than the stars
  And elemental matter. And a cause
Identifying with itself effects debars
  All access to a scrutiny of laws.
  He first philosophized, who dared to pause
Where theorists began their daring flight,
  To know himself, and whence his reason draws
Its cogency to guide the life aright.
So grew Socratic lore; whence Plato's wider sight

XXI.

Of that immortal destiny, which men
   Instinctively for their own being claim.
. And yet, alas, how oft the master's pen
    Becomes bewildered, and his reasons lame,
    Just at the point where needed most to frame
The juncture of an argument, and where
    The soul demands instruction, is his aim
To entertain with Fancy's forms of air.
The student sighed to see how much was lacking there.

XXII.

But while long musing o'er the tangled skein,
   A prior task loomed up before his view.
How should he well discriminate between
    The right and wrong, the fanciful and true?
    What method should the laboring mind pursue
To find the truth, and recognize it found?
    What alchemy distils it?   What the clew,
Which through the mazes of deception wound,
Leads surely to that end?   " And wherefore am I bound

XXIII.

" By force of inward law the truth to know?
   Yea, what is truth, and what is it to me?
May not my life harmoniously flow
    Conformable to all I hear and see,
    Being by nature all that I should be,
And executing all that mortal can,
    Spontaneously, as upward grows the tree?
Nature makes no mistakes.   Then why should man,
Placed so much higher on the wise Creator's plan? "

XXIV.

Let this reply suffice. Why question more?
" Man is a ruler ; and, like God, must rule
By right of law divine; or must deplore
    Himself dethroned, debased—a broken tool,
    Void of significance his life, and full
Of conscience-pangs. To regulate the laws
    Of thousand instincts needs a higher school
Than instinct forms; intelligence which draws
The weight of valid rule from power's profoundest cause.

XXV.

" Hence, deep upon the human soul impressed
    Is the divine necessity to learn
The laws whereby alone it is addressed
    To its life-task, and the command to earn,
    Through life-unfolding study long and stern,
The poise of sovereignty, and sight whereby
    The self-directing spirit may discern
The great exemplar of itself on high,
That it may rule with Him, and His just laws apply."

XXVI.

How vast the care—the thinker's earliest woe—
    To stand amid the thousand things of earth,
And feel that there is there what he must know,
    If he would fill the purpose of his birth,
    And yet possess no measure of their worth :
To think, and think, and ever think in vain ;
    And when he looks for help, to find the dearth
Of clear and settled knowledge among men
Of what the spirit craves, or reason would attain.

XXVII.

" What, must I soar to the divine decree,
    And take my method from the mind of God?
Infallible, most doubtless, would it be,
    Could science ever reach that lofty road.
    Or shall I stoop to the material clod,
And gather up its tedious details,
    That some far distant age may find a broad
Basis for truth, which nothing now avails,
And others may succeed, where all my labor fails ?

XXVIII..

" Or were it not a better way to spin
    One's method from creations of the brain ;
With some fair root of argument begin,
    And thence deducing others, make all plain ?
    Then need no toil be lavished out in vain,
To harmonize, defend, and to unfold
    The mysteries of discord.   Once constrain
The universe into a human mold,
And then its tale is one, consistent, easy told.

XXIX.

" Nay. that were only to impose a scheme
    Of cold deception on the inquiring soul.
Jarring and inconsistent they may seem,
    But facts alone can guide me to my goal.
    Patient I must be : yea, and must control
The gift creative, and its daring pride.
    And whether through the parts I reach the whole,
Or the divine idea is my guide,
Into humility ambition must subside—

XXX.

" Humility, the destined gate for all
    Who in the spirit of true worship come
  Before the shrine of Truth, forever shall
    Forbid the haughty step.   The lofty home
    Of science rises gorgeously, like some
  Majestic minster, spacious and aglow
    With architectural wealth from base to dome,
  But painful the approach, the portal low,
And lowly stoop must they would o'er the threshold go.

.XXXI.

" To know the truth is only from the LORD.
    And he who well his own conceit denies,
  Whether he listens to the written Word,
    Or gathers patiently the mute replies
    Of nature, can alone secure the prize.
  But human fashions, prejudice and pride
    Envelop all with plausible disguise.
  And they who follow them will find supplied
In the wide universe no central stay or guide."

XXXII.

Without a certain method to direct
    Investigation, and to fix its bound,
  Yea, far from any eye that could detect
    The travail of his soul, would Alwyn sound
    Depths within which all effort must be drowned.
  Scheme after scheme he followed but to leave.
    And long he toiled, nor satisfaction found,
  As touching what for truth he must receive,
And of himself and life, and God and heaven believe.

XXXIII.

For 'twas of the originating cause
　Of things in heaven and earth he longed to know,
How they were framed, and by what sovereign laws
　The various currents of their being flow ;
　By what strong energy the living grow,
And why, when life o'er death has won the day,
　It should again surrender to the foe ;
And how it ever can resume its sway
Over the ground thus lost, and wake the dormant clay.

XXXIV.

" Myself am centre of all things to me.
　All things are outward, only I within,
The depths of thought, not what I hear and see,
　But what I am, and shall be, and have been.
　All thoughts must end here, where all thoughts begin.
Yet, like a house of glass, from head to foot,
　My body lets that outward world in,
While this myself sits chemist to transmute
Into the gold of thought the insensate and the brute. .

XXXV.

" This body mine—strange organism, too—
　To outward and to inward both allied,
Myself alike to suffer and to do,
　Yet not myself to reason or decide.
　But where between it and myself divide ?
Myself ! I only change my point of view,
　And then myself is on the outer side :
And I behold it, from a point as true,
A minister whom I must to my use subdue.

XXXVI.

" And yet this self, impalpable, unseen,
    Which flits from soul to body, and anon,
  Swifter than morning's night-dispelling sheen,
    Plants in the soul her citadel alone—
    Incorporate with either or with none,
  Is, after all, the grand reality,
    Whose laws are sciences. All that is known
Is but the sum of her capacity,
Of good the judge, yet source of all iniquity.

XXXVII.

" The unseen is the master, whose mute will
    The laboring limbs implicitly obey.
  And yet I feel there is a greater still,
    To whose invisible, mysterious sway
    I owe allegiance, and whom to gainsay
  Is to indite my own eternal woe.
    But to that greater One the only way
Lies through my inner self, which well to know
Embraces all that man finds noblest here below.

XXXVIII.

' In man's own being is involved the mystery
    Of all existence in things low and high.
  Philosophies, all politics, all history
    In embryo in every bosom lie.
    While mankind lives its past can never die.
  Its continuity no bar divides.
    No age so ancient but its heir am I ;
Nay, one with it, and in me it abides.
One life of man rolls on its long successive tides.

XXXIX.

" All profitless were he whose life should fail
　　To use the present while its moments last ;
But that which lifts him highest on the scale
　　Of being is his knowledge of the past—
　　Capacity to apprehend the vast
Eternal purposes in life that lie,
　　But over which the veil of night is cast,
Save where God grants to patient learner's eye
The backward streaming rays of glory passing by.

XL.

" From inner life all higher life I learn.
　　Man is the only way to God for man,
For through himself alone can man discern
　　. Freedom divine, a ruler and a plan.
　　The infinite he may not—cannot scan,
Nor how the everlasting cycles run,
　　But in his nature sees the Holy One
More than the dew-drop images the sun.
And when God stooped to save, through man the work
　　was done."

XLI.

Yet on no other ground did Alwyn's guides
　　So miserably mock his studious care.
" God is the force which in all things resides,
　　Which germinates in earth and breathes in air."
　" God," said another, " was the when and where
Development commenced its round of laws."
　" God is the all, to make, destroy, repair,
Himself the mass, the change, effect and cause,"
Or " God is man enlarged, as human fancy draws."

XLII.

" Duration is but one—an endless round
   ' Without beginning. So the cause must be
Of all existence. Wheresoever found
   Beginning is not that of Deity.
   . Boundless is space and boundless too is He
Whose purposes to all its realm extend.
   But space, existence, and eternity
I cannot doubt, nor can I comprehend.
So God, however known, all thinking must transcend.

XLIII.

" But if, as some proclaim, there is no God,
   Then that there is a God why did mankind
Ever begin to think ? Were thought a clod,
   Or did brute matter do the work of mind,
   Then why has ever thinking dust resigned
The credit of its thinking ? Why begin
   And occupy, alone and uncombined,
All powers of reason, feeling, sense of sin,
Then think some other life for these to dwell within ?

XLIV.

" Impossible to think an endless line
   Of things which in themselves have each an end ;
Or that existence, of whate'er design,
   Designed itself. Nor can I comprehend
   How nought made something, or could ever tend
To anything ; nor better can conceive
   How God does from eternity descend.
But in Him can implicitly believe,
And without Him can nought as rational receive."

XLV.

'Tis little truly that of God we know ;
　How little of His works which know Him not !
One ray among a thousand serves to throw,
　　Like sunlight through the leaves, a brilliant dot,
　　All else is darkness ; and the bounds of thought
To be extended slowly and with pain.
　　Yea, but the glory of our human lot
It is, however scanty, to retain
Some power of seeing God, exerted not in vain.

XLVI.

As lonely orphan thrown upon the town,
　Without a friend to warn or to defend,
By many a darkling passage may go down
　　Before he learns that whereby to ascend,
　　Unknown the foes with whom he must contend ;
So Alwyn wandered in the world of thought,
　　Toiling for aims which human powers transcend,
Misled by errors speciously taught,
Or seeking truth, where truth is ever vainly sought.

XLVII.

But rightly, wrongly, with or without pain,
　The labor, it was not devoid of joy, .
And in its issue, not always in vain ;
　　Though oft in the procession passing by
　　Before his fancy, men with earnest eye
Darkened as they went on, and sadder grew.
　　Some sank into the earth ; some chose to lie
Gazing on clouds. And some withheld their view
From all except the lines which their own pencils drew.

XLVIII.

It was a daring scheme, and well designed,
  To sum up human knowledge as a whole
In propositions brief and well-defined,
  And thus decide what boundaries control
  The labors and affections of the soul.
And men accepted it, and gravely deemed
  That thought thereby had reached its utmost goal.
The stream they measured ; that from which it streamed,
Eluding measurement, to them as nothing seemed.

XLIX.

Yet they believed that they had fathomed all
  The depths of human nature, and defined,
Down to the last that ever could befall
  One of their race, the mysteries of mind.
  And great philosophers at ease reclined
Upon their laurels, and serenely smiled
  If any one but hinted that behind
Some gleaning of the harvest, straggling wild,
Might still be found unreaped, ungarnered and unpiled.

L.

Nay, all was done, the garner filled and barred.
  Of what the reason could not and it could
The depths had been laid bare, even to the hard
  And earthen floor on which all thinking stood.
  They looked on all their work, and deemed it good.
And what remained ? The heights of heaven to scale,
  And measure God with the same puny rood,
Instruct Him where His strength can best avail,
And where His mighty arm is ever doomed to fail.

5

LI.

Their work seemed gospel, sober truth and sound,
Higher than Revelation to their age.
In it the standard of all truth they found,
In it the touchstone of the sacred page.
A futile war did pious churchmen wage
To save the Word, while siding with its foe,
And yielding all his postulates, engage
His argument too late to overthrow.
As if from upas-seed the wholesome date could grow.

LII.

The reign of Reason, emptily so-called,
Was but the rage of folly and insane
Ambition. The great toiling world, appalled,
Shrunk back upon her steps, as if again
To seek a refuge in the old and vain
Beliefs abandoned long. A stronger foe
Assailed the priests of Reason and their train,
When first from Königsberg came down the blow
Which broke their idol's shrine, and laid his glories low.

LIII.

Fiercely and high the indignant shout arose.
A heretic had dared, profane and bold,
The weakness of their wisdom to expose,
And open richest mines of virgin gold
Beneath the hard foundations of the old
And boasted treasure-house. But time went on.
And onward still the revolution rolled,
Kindling the brave, and the less brave anon,
Till they who shrunk from truth by fashion's plea were
won.

LIV.

But vast as was the bullion of that mine,
  Far from the use of human life it lay.
The hand of Fichté stamped it into coin,
  And sent it forward in the light of day,
  On its ennobling and enriching way ;
Set free the thinking soul and gave it range,
  The objective universe bound to its sway,
And filled it with a mastery glad and strange,
For its own proper ends, o'er every force and change.

LV.

It was a glorious freedom from the bonds
  Which souls so long had been condemned to wear ;
That true enlargement to which joy responds,
  A lofty mount of varied prospects, where
  Exhilaration panted on the air,
And a new life infused the thrilling veins.
  Grant it a dream, 'twas one divinely fair,
And opening supernatural domains
In heaven and earth, in seas and hills and plains.

LVI.

The old philosophy was tried and doomed,
  The inherent force of mind installed anew.
Imagination had her right resumed,
  And feeling dawned once more into a true
  Integral power.   Disciples not a few
. Followed his steps with scarce inferior sway.
  Broad was the cloud-land which young Schelling drew,
Grand in its masses undefined and grey,
Unfolding life in death, and nurture in decay.

LVII.

Hegel, with intuition strong and keen,
　　Pierced to the core of things, and grasped their mold,
Presumed by the unseen to judge the seen,
　　And all its contents to describe and hold ;
　　The master-spirit most complete and bold,
Who framed for thoughtful Germany the new
　　Philosophy, which taking in the old,
And harmonizing all the structure, drew
That confidence which should be granted to the true.

LVIII.

It moved a tempest o'er the world of thought,
　　From the deep heart of Germany, in France
And England with contending currents fought,
　　And many a stubborn rock of circumstance,
　　Which multitudes beheld with timid glance ;
And fields of earing grain and rustling corn
　　Were prostrate laid before its dread advance.
And clouds of. dust upon its wings were borne.
Yet health was in its train, and clearer shone the morn.

LIX.

And when it passed, the dust fell back to earth,
　　The angry thunders muttered to repose.
The prostrate maize received another birth,
　　And in the strength of richer life arose,
　　And breaking clouds did fairer heavens disclose.
The new philosophy, behind her blame,
　　Carried a truth to vanquish shallower foes.
Perhaps she fully earned her evil fame ;
But, through the Father's love, good of that evil came.

LX.

Yet good all other than what men designed,
    And all upon another level done,
More varied powers, and wider range of mind,
    And ground for faith and hope were nobly won.
    But of the structure thus so well begun,
The crowning members seemed of vapor made,
    Flitting as mists beneath the morning sun.
New masters still new world-plans displayed,
Alike illusive all, and doomed alike to fade.

LXI.

The keynote of the universe, which holds
    All its deep harmonies in true accord—
The master-plan, which in its grasp enfolds
    Matter and law, infinity, the Word,
    With all its branching lines of power explored,
To grasp in measurements of human thought,
    Was the vast height to which the teacher soared.
What wonder if aspiring Reason wrought
Sometimes in vain, and back deceitful trophies brought?

LXII.

Men, who could think the Cosmos thus revealed,
    Squandered what seemed exhaustless wealth away.
That wealth a soberer purpose yet shall wield,
    Which spendthrift Fancy shall not lead astray.
    A new philosophy shall yet array
All truths the Transcendentalist can boast,
    With all that hold their place from earlier day,
In harmony, one vast organic host
Of lessons old and new, which mankind value most.

LXIII.

Thank God for all the health was in the storm,
  And thanks to God the storm is passed and gone.
. O'er what it did to waste and to deform
  'Twere profitless to grumble or bemoan.
Better it were did blessings come alone,
But if with war in all its dread array,
  Still thanks to him by whom the good is done;
Nor thanks the less, if on the triumph day
The ranks were broken up, the weapons cast away.

LXIV.

But is this science—feeling in the dark,
  Each for himself, the best that he can find,
Without a common principle or mark,
  The sheaves of all the harvest field to bind,
  Thus every workman after his own mind
Building his castle in the earth or air,
  Out of the mass to which he has consigned
Some earlier structure no less proudly fair?
Oh, speculation, what your settled truth, and where?

LXV.

There is philosophy which smooths the path
  To knowledge—lucid thinking of the wise—
There is philosophy, a rod of wrath,
  In whose corrupt but specious disguise
  The truth evaporates, and virtue dies.
There is philosophy, a verbal clothing
  Of shallow thought, which at the surface lies,
And wastes its thin vitality in frothing—
Nonsense philosophy, which leads, at best, to nothing.

LXVI.

How poorly learned the lesson—the rich dower,
  Great son of Sophroniscus, left by thee —
That the best power of scheming is not power
  Of knowing, and however fair may be
  The system reared by proud Philosophy
Beyond the limits of what man can know,
  'Tis but a fabric framed of phantasy.
Nor owns it aught of all the glittering show
Which was not carried up from soberer realms below.

LXVII.

Unwavering faith in Nature, fullest trust
  In common things, their kindred and their force,
In the pure truth of air, and light, and dust,
  Must be the clew wherewith to thrid our course
  Through mysteries of being.   Sole resource
For erring man is to accept the hand
  Of the great Author of the universe.
His only are the lessons to command
Conviction of all minds which truly understand.

LXVIII.

For that within us is not merely ours
  Whereby we know, distinguish and combine.
From all eternity those glorious powers
  Have energized the same in the divine
  Nature, as now, with feebler force, in mine.
Down through duration have they urged their flight,
  Filling the universe with their design.
And every work of God, unveiled to sight
Fits into human thought, as native, true, and right.

LXIX.

Well-ordered thinking seeing clearly through
    The changing mass and outward forms of things,
Taking the everlasting from the new,
    The growths of being from their vital springs,
    To deathless principles its labor brings ;
And these builds into system by the law
    Of mental nature's soundest reasonings.
So apprehend we God, with solemn awe,
· And thence, for human life, familiar lessons draw.

LXX.

The clearest thinkers, and the most profound,
    Though far apart in time and place they be,
Think most alike.   And on their wisest ground
    With them the soberer multitude agree.
    Thus ever with the great Hellenic three
Must all partake who think complete and true—
    With the Lyceum or Academy,
Or him from whose pelucid springs they drew.
Thus, in the best, the old still animates the new.

LXXI.

And what did Alwyn of his labor gain,
    His eager converse with the wise of old,
That lofty counsel, which so often ta'en
    Night after night he would return to hold ?
    Gain of an intellectual wealth untold,
Of nobler worth to the immortal spirit
    Than all the veins of Californian gold—
Treasures which perish not, which they inherit,
Who claim not on the right of geniture, but merit.

LXXII.

Wide vision of the fair, material earth,
Perceptions of a new and varied kind,
Which, though of outward objects, have their birth
  In unseen intercourse of mind with mind,
  Conceptions of the heavenly spark enshrined
In human flesh, and in its types of things,
  Which toil untutored dare not hope to find,
With feeling's tenderest glow and deepest springs,
And Reason's firmest tread, and Fancy's lightest wings.

LXXIII.

Rich mines of thought, yielding for daily use,
  The current coin of virtues, lovely, pure,
The clue of principle for the abstruse,
  And lenses to enlighten the obscure,
  Far-reaching laws, which ever must endure,
The arbiters of pleasure and of pain,
  To guide the reason and the heart assure.
While forms of beauty flitted round his brain,
Like birds of Paradise, in long succeeding train.
  5*

CANTO FIFTH.

ANALYSIS.

CANTO FIFTH.

I.

WHOEVER would the heights of truth attain
   Must pass the ordeal of doubt and dread,
Go out into the desert, and sustain
   Temptations of the Devil, and must tread
   Them under foot, crushing the serpent's head ;
Of his own heart the treasures must explore,
   And choose the guide by whom he will be led
By path or trodden or untrod before,
But once for all decide his aim to change no more.

II.

Such Sacred Writ declares the will of Heaven,
   Such fate the nations to their great assign.
Such the example by the Saviour given.
   The ordeal of temptation his divine
   Being, though spotless, did not choose decline.
Through such a horror of great darkness all,
   Predestined with a brighter ray to shine,
Must pass to their vocation. 'Tis the pall
Which covers, as with death, what life must not recall.

III.

Young life is but a prelude.   Now begins
  The great dramatic action.   Born again,
Victorious over weaknesses or sins
  Are all the mightiest workers among men—
  The prophet heroes, whose far-seeing ken
Directs the march of ages.   Moses knew
  The trials of the desert ere his pen
The solemn wonders of Jehovah drew.
And through the wastes of doubt the faith of Luther
    grew.

IV.

Men argue to convince, or to defend ;
  They reach their thoughts by more mysterious ways.
Upon the silent steps of use depend
  Opinions which fill up their common days ;
  While intuition, with one fervid gaze,
Transcends the realm where common laborers plod ;
  One deadly struggle with the Fiend displays
The painful path by hero footsteps trod,
Transforming to the heart one interview with God.

V.

But not through ecstacy of inner light,
  Not by a miracle, nor in a dream,
Did Alwyn pass the boundaries of night
  To meet the fervor of the rising beam.
  Graver the toil, more distant the extreme
Assigned his weary feet, by teachers led
  Who seemed the teachers of the truth to him.
Friends whom he loved, and books which he had read
With trust, across his way the dreary desert spread.

VI.

And thus, as every soul of man must stand,
　Alwyn before the gates of science stood,
Left to himself, without a helping hand,
　Surrounded by a boundless solitude,
　As much alone, in choice of ill or good,
As if the earth were desert.　He had known
　In common cares what tender friendship could,
But life's great trials must be undergone
Where friends can never come, in the soul's depths alone.

VII.

'Twas not a conflict between work and play,
　Nor yet for him had indolence a charm ;
But magic Art led in her witching sway
　A spirit quick to know, a bosom warm
　With genial love to every line and form
And hue of beauty ; while to learning still,
　Whose varied work had done so much to arm
Him for life's war, he clung with grateful will,
And science could alone his highest wishes fill—

VIII.

His highest wishes to secure that truth
　Which man from Nature in herself can wring.
Crude facts, in the habiliments uncouth,
　In which from hard experiment they spring—
　The crucible, the anvil, the harsh ring
Of formulas of logic moved disgust
　To high-toned lore; and Art, whose dainty wing
Spurns the slow feet which labor with the dust ;
Yet there he deemed must man repose his firmest trust.

IX.

'Twas not a matter which the will could solve
 By simple choice ; as erst, when Greece was young,
Did on the doubting Hercules devolve,
 But one which earnest thought and purpose strong,
 And self-examination practiced long,
And large attainment pondered deep and pressed
 Into the very life, as right or wrong,
Alone can settle to the soul's behest
With judgment upon which the choice will ever rest.

X.

" But to that end, my soul herself must know,
 The native purpose of her life must see—
What talents did the Almighty Lord bestow,
 What must the occupancy of them be,
 And how my wishes with my powers agree.
Science must find her origin and guide
 As outward things reflect themselves in me.
And thus shall Art be the most truly tried,
And Learning's largest wealth most wisely be applied."

XI.

All true Philosophy must needs include
 Intrinsically a religious soul,
Not, of necessity, as pure or good,
 But such as energizes in the whole
 Career, and gives in judgment at the goal.
And yet how oft, alike in new and old,
 We feel a dark insidious control,
With the connected system, fold on fold
Enwrap us with its coils, all stealthily and cold.

XII.

And oft, as Alwyn read, and thought and read,
  The argument seemed sure, though into doubt
Leading the heart, bewildering as it led.
  Something was wrong. But where, within, without,
  In him, or in creation round about?
Or in religion, as its tale was told?
  He sought to plant himself with trust devout
On Holy Scripture. But his faith, cajoled
By some strange hidden charm, though grasping, failed
    to hold.

XIII.

And ever, as he felt for surer ground,
  He lost the sense of that whereon he trod;
While ever echoed from the dark profound
  " Is this indeed the very word of God?
  Has that Almighty One, whose sovereign nod
Rules orbs and orbits with resistless sway,
  Whose being through the universe abroad
Pervades all space, as light pervades the day,
Confided His decrees to creatures formed of clay?"

XIV.

In vain he questions of the sacred leaves
  By aid of speculations which pretend
That every heart the indwelling·God receives,
  And all His attributes in each descend.
  Not thus the mystery can be explained.
For then the prophet only wrote his own.
  And who shall know when inspiration fanned
The lyric light and fire, and when alone
The bard's creative thought, the lyre's enrapturing tone?

XV.

As in the dawn of Greece among the isles
  Which gem the bosom of the Ægean sea,
When there still reigned the beauty which beguiles
  The captive spirit into ecstacy,
  In moments of exalted reverie,
The bard held converse with the world unseen,
  And glowing thoughts flashed into life which he
Had labored not with argument to glean
From aught that previous life or outward things could
    mean,

XVI.

Emotions dawned unsought, and visions came
  In long array, a world of living things,
And language kindled after them like flame,
  While all unknown to him their several springs.
  He from the god, who o'er his climate flings
Its robe of beauty, deemed the treasure given,
  Claimed inspiration for imaginings
For which his soul unconsciously had striven.
And hence Apollo's harp, the Muse, the poet's heaven.

XVII.

And should the prophet's inspiration be
  Such as infused the Chian bard of old,
Or from fair Paros•sent the elegy,
  Or taught the Lesbian melic art, or rolled
  The dithyramb in many a doubling fold,
Though high the thought, melodious the line,
  No claim upon conviction can he hold
Which he might not as well to Greece resign,
And David's, Pindar's harp are equally divine.

XVIII.

With such array of questions to be solved,
    The earnest seeker turned again, again,
To sage expounders, and in thought revolved
    The divers views and varying faith of men
    Who drew from the same book their creeds; and when
He saw their fierce and unforgiving zeal,
    In life, in death, with voice, with sword and pen,
For doctrines of that book, dark doubts would steal
Upon him of its claims to govern or reveal.

XIX.

Alas, that ministers of Truth should doom
    To doubt the spirit longing to believe,
Or deepen question into sceptic gloom,
    For those who of their sceptic questions grieve,
    That disputants confuted may receive
The shackles of a faith that binds the will.
    To Alwyn's heart the sense would ever cleave
Of guilt in thinking false. Nor could he still
That craving of the soul which truth alone can fill.

XX.

" If I must question Scripture, is there aught
    Of greater certainty? Has any mind
Seen deeper into Deity, and brought
    To light instructions of a surer kind?
    To him would my convictions be resigned.
I must presume, if learnéd men and wise
    Reject the Scripture, 'tis because they find
A better wisdom than within it lies
Elsewhere, which Reason neither questions nor denies;

XXI.

" Or questions less ; or otherwise they deem
 Some argument refuting it in mass
As more than it entitled to esteem.
  'Twere wisest then to learn from him who has
  Possession of the truths which so surpass,
And thereby settle, once for all, the best.
  Why suffer doubts my spirit to harass,
If truth accessible has stood the test ?
I would it know forthwith, and there forever rest.

XXII.

" If mankind grows in wisdom as in age,
 As men, judged wisest of the race, maintain,
In true development from stage to stage,
  Truth must become progressively more plain,
  And every step in thinking be a gain.
Why for instruction toilsomely descend
  To the far depths of time, there to remain
In earlier progress, when I may command
The last results upon the level where I stand."

XXIII.

Man was not constituted to repose
 In unbelief. Essential to his peace
Is faith. Investigation cannot close
  Until the struggling spirit win release
  From bonds of doubt, and vacillation cease.
'Twill grasp at every semblance of the true,
  Perceiving trust in the untrue decrease,
And Alwyn for support with ardor flew
To seize the mask of truth the Deist held to view.

XXIV.

And did he not a purer light receive
From reverential Herbert? . Nothing more
Than the departing rays of daylight leave—
A twilight falling faint and fainter o'er
Succeeding toilers in that helpless lore,—
Twilight which darkened as the march went on.
Proud Bolingbroke a showy garment wore,
And much he boasted, lofty was the tone
Of his supreme contempt on Holy Scripture thrown.

XXV.

But daring ignorance betrayed itself
In ludicrous exposure to the eye
Fresh from inspection of what on the shelf
The noble lord had suffered long to lie.
Reckless assertions, which but few would try
To verify, among the few who could,
On which the haughty peer seemed to rely,
The careful scholar thoughtfully reviewed,
And left the noble lord in no respectful mood.

XXVI.

But he had ceased to blend men with the cause
Which they defend, and promptly did repair
To other sources, where extreme applause
Appeared to indicate more solid ware.
From France the loud acclaim, which rent the air,
Came in the tone of triumph. And it gave
To every breeze thy boasted name, Voltaire.
What though they crowned thee only for the grave,
Thou won'st the highest meed thy agéd heart could
    crave.

XXVII.

With what a glow of joy did Alwyn bend
    Over the volumes of that far-famed man.
What might he not expect from him whose end
    Was proud as the long, brilliant race he ran—
From him whom nations honored, and whom one
Adored and followed whereso'er he led,
    Whose pen had matched the monarchies; the plan
Of whose campaigns of innovation bred
Hope that the despot's rule, and falsehood's night had
    fled.

XXVIII.

He looked expectant to the boasted chief.
    The arguments that swayed a nation, must
Surely avail to lend his mind relief.
    Alas, how feeble was that nation's trust.
    Not Sodom's apple crumbling into dust
At touch of hungry pilgrim, not the reed
    As shelter from the tempest's angry gust,
So ill requite dependent in his need.
In theory how fair; how terrible. in deed.

XXIX.

The pictured reign benign of Reason lay
    Before the admiring eye. A fairy land,
Where all abuses should be swept away,
    And Virtue, by the breath of Freedom fanned,
    Should bloom in perfect beauty, 'neath the wand
Of the magician rose; yet distant far,
    And to be reached but by a bloody hand.
The present still was unrelenting war.
And his own Eden seemed to be the battle-car.

XXX.

His power was to demolish, and his aim
   To scathe and blast pretension. And right well
He occupied his talent. Sword and flame
   Devoured around him, and his vengeance fell
   Where Justice crushed did righteously rebel,
And reason claimed redress. But in the fight,
   Led with such skill and valor, did he tell
The anxious souls he could so well excite
To hatred of the wrong, where they might find the right?

XXXI.

Yet deists had their architect of schemes,
   And fair full oft were the designs he drew.
And such the tints in which he robed his themes,
   That even they who felt constrained to view
   The whole chimerical, half wished it true.
If ever truth from grace of style could grow,
   Conviction from expression's force accrue,
The deist's faith prosperity should know
From thy constructive art and eloquence, Rousseau.

XXXII.

Then what the better wisdom he arrayed
   Against the ancient Scripture? "A divine
Foreseeing power, which is to be obeyed,
   Of providence and purposes benign,
   A life to come, and punishment condign
Of those who sin, and blessing for the just."
   Is that the better way—thus to decline
A loving Saviour's grace, and blindly trust
A cold device of state, as loyal subject must?

XXXIII.

And yet there was a hero in the man,
   Who, in a time of violence and lies,
When Church and State alike imposed their ban
   On words that touched the hem of their disguise,
   When mankind's best, its truthful and its wise,
Were crushed to earth by privileged insolence,
   Could strip Hypocrisy to common eyes,
And lay her bare in all her rank offence,
Unawed by vengeful Power's malignant recompense.

XXXIV.

Ah, gallant France, how deeply didst thou bleed
   That freedom from untruth to realize !
Shrunk not from mental toil nor daring deed,
   Nor vast expenditure of sacrifice,
   So thou might'st win the long-contested prize—
So reason might the mastery attain,
   And rule in nature's true and simple guise
Emancipate from despots.   And thy gain ?
Writ upon Russian snows, and Leipsic's dreadful plain.

XXXV.

To students of the truth must not the voice
   Of even a nation be the sovereign guide,
Nor give a bias to conclusive choice.
   It seems as if a matter must be tried
   With fairness where so many minds decide.
But of the millions who record the vote,
   How few have ever, for one hour, relied
On Reason's light ?   Some leading mind they quote,
Tread blindly in his steps, and speak his words by rote.

XXXVI.

The multitude are creatures of their times.
　　And times that stir the waters of the mind,
Fertile alike in virtues and in crimes,
　　Though times when noblest men their places find,
　　Oft bring to surface things of meanest kind,
And often public weakness, in its need,
　　Will blindly follow those, who also blind,
Are foremost but as far as they exceed
In wildness of design and recklessness of deed.

XXXVII.

A few strong thinkers, and the boldest first,
　　Are always found a nation's intellect.
They may be men accurséd with the thirst
　　Of power and fortune, or they may reject
　　All selfish gain, the public to effect ;
But on those few the mass will still depend,
　　At least until their purposes are wrecked—
Success must aye the favorite defend—
But if one leader sinks, another must ascend.

XXXVIII.

Thus, in the suffrages that crowned Voltaire,
　　We read no real addition to the weight
Of his opinions.　For the voters were
　　The populace, upon whose will that great
　　And active spirit held the rod of fate,
And not because their reasonings had proved
　　The justness of his views ; but from their state
Of natural dependence, as behooved
Them 'neath his clearer thought, and stronger will they
　　moved.

6

XXXIX.

But Alwyn sought for truth, not domination,
  Not exposition sole of the untrue
Could satisfy his ardent expectation,
  Awakened by the crowds that leader drew.
  No pleasantries could turn aside his view.
No satire the most witty, not the play
  Of liveliest fancy, ever yielding new
Creations of amusement now could stay
The earnest heart, which sought, through doubt, its
    darkling way.

XL.

One hope remained.   Still might he not presume,
  With him who bore the philosophic name,
The calm, the subtle, unimpassioned Hume,
  On whom reposed such men of learnéd fame,
  To find that best, so long his unseen aim?
Ah, now, 'twas disappointment's deeper deep.
  And ere to the concluding page he came,
He felt despair upon his spirit creep.
Defeat had led to rage, but sorrow chose to weep—

XLI.

To weep over the weakness of mankind,
  His own discomfiture and hopes decayed,
The weakness of the wise, who could be blind
  To the poor sophisms upon them played
  By one whom their own theories had made
Of more importance than his argument,
  Utterly void of any thing to aid
A troubled spirit, earnestly intent
To know that good in which this life were wisest spent.

XLII.

" Is this thy growth, Philosophy ?   Have I
　　Come from the teachings of a distant age,
　From Aristotle, Zeno, and the high
　　Instructions of the Academic sage,
　　In fruitless speculation to engage
　With barren doubt ?   And is it thus appears
　　Thy champion most valiant war to wage ?"
　In sooth, it was abundant cause for tears
That largely boasted gain of twice a thousand years.

XLIII.

And yet the world admired.   The gift of style,
　　Easy and polished, although cold and thin,
　A superficial age might well beguile ;
　　But what did learnéd doctors find therein
　　So hard to master, and so high to win,
　So difficult to answer, where in wrong ?
　　'Tis easy, when with error all begin,
　For the consistent false to seem the strong,
And over partial truth to boast the victory long.

XLIV.

'Twere profitless to further trace his way,
　　Pursued in hopelessness and closed in pain,
　And followed but because no other lay
　　Before him yet more hopeful or more plain,
　　Among the honest theorists but vain,
　Who built for France the systems crude and wild
　　Which only bore to ruin the mad train
　Of headlong revolutionists, self-styled
Philosophers, until their words no more beguiled.

XLV.

For all alike evinced it their chief end
 To overthrow conviction that the Word
Of God was in the Jewish books contained,
 While futile every effort to afford
 Instructions which more justly might accord
With human faith, and honestly unmask
 The real replies to questions which the lord
Of this creation cannot choose but ask.
Their end was unbelief. And therein closed their task.

XLVI.

" Is unbelief the utmost, then, that man
 Is destined to arrive at here below ?
And is he doomed to moral life, who can
 No principle of moral judgment know ?
 Does the Great Author of all justice throw
His creatures forth into a moral night,
 And punish them for wandering ? Does he show,
To guide their way, no ray of heavenly light,
Condemn them for the wrong, and yet not teach the
  right ?"

XLVII.

Yet one bold fact was ever clear. Of all
 The volumes out of which he counsel took,
The only one to fully meet the call
 Of his inquiries was the Jewish book.
 By what authority it dared to look
Into the heart and offer such replies,
 Plain, searching to the spirit's inmost nook,
Must be determined in some other wise ;
But answers, true or false, it surely did comprise.

XLVIII.

And then what mighty names, from age to age,
  The history of its victories adorn,
The clear logician, the profoundest sage
    Of independent reason, who would scorn
    The sophist's empty trade, alike have worn
Themselves by toil to make its lessons clear,—
  · But has not intellect the fetters borne
Of every creed?   And does the task appear
So easy to reject what youth has learned to fear?

XLIX.

Did Solon's faith his native gods resign,
    Or cancel rites he could not reconcile?
Great minds have bent before Minerva's shrine,
    Adored the Ganges and the sacred Nile,
    Looked to Olympian peaks and Delos isle;
Nay, upon Indian and Egyptian plains,
    Prostrate to objects most obscene and vile,
  . Have poured the earnest prayer.   What then remains?
To grant the truth of all that intellect sustains?

L.

" 'Tis little in the scale, when one would weigh
    The worth of an opinion, right or wrong,
To have for either side the claim to lay
    That it has been defended by the strong.
    Not unto human power such rights belong.
The greatest minds have furthest gone astray.
    And prejudices linger oft among
The clearest views, and wield a secret sway
Where freest will is strong, and would the least obey.

LI.

" Reason alone must judge of true and false,
　.Each soul of man its own decision make.
　And where it proves incompetent, nought else
　　Can here below the labor undertake.
　　Dreadful responsibility ! to stake
　One's everlasting welfare on the chance
　　Of right conclusion, where so many wake
　Too late to error and its recompense.
Yet here must knowledge end, here terminate advance.

LII.

" For grant the claim that the Supreme has given
　　A revelation to the sons of men,
　Laden with wisdom and the grace of Heaven,
　　On which they safely may rely.　What then ?
　　Which one is truly the inspired pen ?
　Which is of God ?　The Hebrew prophet's lore ?
　　Egyptian Thoth ?　The sage whose prudent ken
　The crowded millions of Sinim adore ;
Or who the Vedas sung, long lost in distant yore ?

LIII.

" Vain problem : ' By their fruit shall they be known.'
　　A scheme professed of human blessing can
　Evince a source divine by good alone
　　Performed in those who follow out its plan.
　　And what if critics, who the closest scan
　These many works, should find them all divine ?
　　Must the Creator speak but once to man
　And all His favor to one tribe confine ?
Must truths to falsehood turn whene'er they thus com-
　　bine ?

LIV.

" Such were strange alchemy." So Alwyn saw,
  And soon abandoned the pursuit which no
Investigation could avail to draw
    To fit conclusion. Whither should he go
    To find the Sibyl's leaves; or who can show
The books of Thoth; or if one may ascend
    To source of the Avesta, or to know
The faith in which the Vedic hymns were penned,
What hope that toil should thus attain a happier end?

LV.

" Poorly adapted to such themes as these
  Is the brief time to mortal works supplied.
To scrutinize the Sanscrit and Chinese
    Is doubtless worth the scholar's honest pride;
    But if the truth was ever thus descried,
Its gain to human life must ill repay
    The toil of finding, if so long applied,
It has not yielded other fruits to-day
Than those which China's hordes and Hindu castes dis-
    play.

LVI.

" Is there a creed mankind can *not* believe?
    Or is there aught beyond the range of doubt?
To smooth the way for what they would receive,
    Or rule the truthful, when offensive, out,
    There is no evidence men cannot scout.
Nature full oft beholds her facts denied,
    Her hosts of demonstration put to rout.
Nor has the love of God a word supplied
On which the varying minds of men will not divide."

LVII.

Amid the agitation and unrest
  Awakened by the winds of unbelief,
A gust of strange, wild joy would heave his breast—
  A turbid exultation of relief—
  A fierce vain-glory, bursting through the grief
Of failure, while he seemed to comprehend
  Within the circle of his view the chief
Defenders of the Word, and in the end
Of proofs to see the want of all they would defend.

LVIII.

Like a breakwater to the stormy main,
  Would a strong argument sometimes restore
His faith ; until along the billowy plain
  Rushed bolder lines of surge upon the shore,
  And with defiance, and insultant roar,
Like charge of heroes hastening to the fray,
  Would headlong o'er his strongest bulwarks pour,
Tossing in pride their feathery crests of spray,
And scattering his defence, like pebbles, on their way.

LIX.

" And who shall tell," he bitterly inquires,
  " What are the certain seals of sacred writ?
How shall I know the doctrine God inspires,
  And be prepared, as arbiter, to sit
  In judgment on its virtues to outfit
My spirit for communion of the blest?
  Is there a mark on language to transmit
Its proof of birth in God ?   Or does all rest
On subtler evidence, whose truth eludes my quest ?

LX.

' And by whose judgment were it safe to mete
  The holy oracles of God withal ?
Nay, were men's unanimity complete,
  Is there no doubt, while captive in the thrall
  Of sinful nature, that what men may call
Most holy, with a view of truth so slim
  As not to fully comprehend the small,
Will be received as holiest by Him
Whose eye pervades the vast, nor to the small is dim ?

LXI.

" Then, let it pass how men began to be,
  By whom created, on whatever wise.
Behold the sum of all his history,
  He rules the creatures, and himself, and dies.
  And whosoever curiously pries
Into what follows, or has gone before,
  Will hear from the far distance, as replies,
The echoes of his questions.   Nothing more
Has answered human call, from that mysterious shore.

LXII.

" There is no proof that there is aught to prove,
  No certainty in evidence is shown.
For proof needs proof ; and then it must behoove
  To find at last a place for umpire's throne."
  Alwyn dismissed his queries with a groan.
To what result had boasted reason led ?
  To this grand truth that nothing can be known.
Earth was a blank, emotion's self was dead.
And round his hopeless soul a mental midnight spread.

  6*

LXIII.

Pale with repeated vigils by the lamp,
    And worn with cares, which sooner sap the flow
Of life's warm current than the deck, the camp,
    Or any toil the animal can know—
    Those sceptic clouds, which round the spirit throw
Their deepening shadows, until reason fails,
    Where doubts on doubts, mysteries on mysteries grow,
To penetrate the uncertainty that veils
The sources of all peace, the life of God assails.

LXIV.

Into a grove of old and solemn gloom
    He wandered heedless where his steps might wend,
So might he but escape the fearful doom
    To which his reeling reason seemed to tend.
    And holy Nature, like a loving friend,
Received him to her arms, and in his ear
    Poured those sad, sighing tones, which best descend
Upon the troubled heart, to soothe and cheer,
While leaving undisturbed the solitude so dear.

LXV.

Turning his eyes on high, he gazed awhile
    Along the spangled canopy of night,
Till those fair orbs that ever seem to smile
    All tranquilly, untroubled by the blight
    Of human hopes, as if their distant light
Were not created for a world of woe,
    Insensibly shed on his mental sight
A portion of their own calm, steady glow
Unchanging in itself, though clouds may roll below.

LXVI.

That spiritual war is always gain
  Which manfully and truthfully is fought.
Defeat full oft, in battles of the brain,
  Brings better spoil than ever victory brought.
  The haughty triumph of successful thought
Parches with pride the surface of the soul,
  Till sowing and all culture come to nought,
And sunshine without cloud enwraps the whole
In poverty of drought no sunshine can console.

LXVII.

'Tis sometimes well that weeping clouds should spread
  Their gloomy pall across the beaming sky.
'Tis sometimes well, with aching heart and head,
  That one should see his dearest prospects die.
  Full oft the failures which our hopes deny,
Are forces of deep verity and right,
  A barren confidence to mortify,
To drive the ploughshare, with relentless might,
Through life, and bring its best fertility to light.

CANTO SIXTH:

ANALYSIS.

CANTO VI.—Philosophical studies, delightful as they are in themselves, are shorn of their highest profit if pursued to the
neglect of social duties—Alwyn turns from speculation to
practical things—Importance of sympathy with men to the
completeness of the individual—Certain doctrines proved by
having always actuated mankind—Human nature—Alwyn re-
volts from his experience in business life—Without a faith
established in God, he loses faith in man—Nature has lost her
former charms—A dream, sleep has her own world.

CANTO SIXTH.

I.

FOR the rich flow of far-pervading thought,   [hour,
   Which comes strong, deep and clear, at midnight's
To patient thinking could the world be bought,
   Who would conclude the purchase—for a power
   O'er things of clay would sacrifice the dower
Of the All-wise, which constitutes him lord
   Of unseen realms, from whose exhaustless store
Enjoyments nobler than earth can afford
More kindred to the soul are ever round him poured?

II.

And yet there is a sadness in the bliss
   Even of those rushing thoughts, as if behind
There lay concealed a deeper source than this
   Of intellectual triumph, which the mind
   Dimly perceives far off, and undefined,
And knows to be essential to her peace,
   But which she strives in vain to grasp and bind
Unto herself, till humbled efforts cease,
Despondency invades, and weary hopes decrease.

III.

For, with the multitude of thoughts that live
    And have their active being among men,
O'er which the reason can avail to give
    The practical dominion of the pen,
    Dim forms of glorious truth will come, and then
Depart, as shadows of the clouds flit by,
    'Neath Summer's sun, not to return again,
But fire the soul with rapture while they fly,
As harbingers of things to be revealed on high.

IV.

The mists of doubt, at times, will pass along,
    And shade the ideal prospect for a day.
And he who seeks the truth may labor long,
    Warring with countless errors on his way.
    But persevering valor will repay
With triumph in the end; while the hard toil
    Expended in the war confers a sway
O'er powers of thought all future foes to foil,
For which alone 'twere well he spent the midnight oil.

V.

It is, indeed, a banquet of the soul,
    Thus to transcend our prison-house of mold,
And as a portion merge in the great whole
    Of spiritual being, and to hold
    Communion with the mighty minds of old,
And with the dwellers of the vast unseen
    And sacred realms, where rest to man untold,
The plans of God, as if one stood between
Earth and the springs of all that shall be and has been.

VI.

But man has duties to perform on earth.
　　And even the proudest efforts of his mind
Must take their turn with things of meaner birth.
　　Not wholly dust, nor all a soul, designed
　　To fill a middle place, where both combined
May share in equal tasks, he feels a call
　　To active labors, helpful to mankind ;
Yet not beneath his heavenly source to fall.
Hard is his task who seeks to know and practice all.

VII.

The middle watch of night had now passed by,
　　When Alwyn turned him from the fruitless pain
Of reconciling what must ever lie
　　Unreconciled to him whose thoughts contain
　　Less than the universe.　" 'Tis also vain
To trust to other eyes, when I may look
　　On the same sources, and perhaps to gain
A certainty whence these my teachers took
Their most bewildering doubts," he said, and shut his
　　book.

VIII.

" The natural is real ; or, if not so,
　　As good as real to us, who ever lie
Under necessity in all we do,
　　Whatever we may·credit or deny,
　　Whatever ends we seek or means employ,
In every act and purpose, not insane,
　　To deal with it as such.　And they who try
To treat it as unreal will try in vain,
Self-contradicted still, with all their care and pain.

IX.

" And if it is impossible to live
    Consistently with doubt, then doubt must be
Unreasonable ; and they who choose to give
    Their confidence to Nature full and free,
    With the demands of reason best agree.
Forces preceding reason guide our hands,
    And dictate reason's fundamental plea.
And to submit to those constraining bands
Are all alike constrained by reason's own demands."

X.

But then arose, what oft arose before
    In dim impression, now in clearest light,
What to the moral being ever more
    Import than question of the true and right,
    Yet taking both within their range of sight,
The solemn heights of Duty. " What am I,
    Amid these wonders of creative might,
And what the part assigned me by the High
And Holy One, who writes His will in earth and sky ?

XI.

" Mighty is *truth*—the everlasting law
    Of God's own nature, and thereby the key
To all the world of mysteries that draw
    Existence from His purpose—and to be .
    Conformed to which is *right ;* but of the three
Duty is ours ; for us must ever span
    The sum of highest knowledge. Well to see,
Backward and forward and throughout, the plan
Of one's own work, and do it, must be ever most to man.

˙XII.

Deep study and much reading had supplied
  Knowledge, though partial, of the highest things.
That theoretic learning, to which pride
  Of intellect forever fondly clings,
  Alwyn had quaffed at its profoundest springs.
But true experience, though a path less smooth,
  Has much to teach that reading never brings.
For to the warm imaginings of youth
A transcendental haze enrobes the simplest truth.

XIII.

The agony of long-protracted doubt
  And toilsome study oftentimes restrain
And chill the feelings. Yet if truth shines out
  They burst forth fresh, rejoicing in her train.
  But he who would direct from nature gain
And read the science of the human heart,
  Shall often be compelled to suffer pain
That will not lightly from his soul depart,
Lasting as wisdom's ground, and as the price of Art.

XIV.

For he must feel, not merely sympathize,
  In all the common joys and pains of men.
Nay, not their petty whims must he despise,
  Share in their follies and regrets, and then
  Study must still be wedded to his ken,
The springs of action rightly to unfold.
  But he who trusts to the recluse's pen,
Which can but aid, shall never see unrolled
One tithe of the great truths in human nature told.

XV.

To Alwyn's mind 'twas observation solely
　　Which now appeared as hopeful. "Surely he
Who looks on Wisdom's working and on folly,
　　And treasures up whate'er the lesson be,
　　Must the first springs of human action see,
And learn the secrets of this wondrous frame,
　　Where God is sovereign and where man is free,
The cause of suffering and the source of blame,
Life's various motives, and their ever common aim."

XVI.

Such were the hopes in whose deceitful light
　　He now the outline of his course designed.
Fields, as it seemed to him, unreaped, but white
　　Unto the harvest, opened to his mind,
　　Fruitful of expectations from mankind.
. And the romance, which buoyant Fancy threw
　　Over adventure yet untried, combined
With all to lend attraction to the view,
Which now before him lay, unlimited and new.

XVII.

" Have not the martyred multitudes that lie
　　Along the pathway of two thousand years,
Confirmed the creed for which they chose to die ?
　　Or have they vainly shed their blood and tears,
　　Endured privation, vanquished human fears,
And triumphed over death ? Nay, let me found
　　My faith upon the basis which appears
Sustained by evidence so large and sound.
Man knows no higher faith, and faith no higher ground."

XVIII.

Thus pondering long the doctrines and the views
  Which crowded for admission on his sight,
'Mong which he carefully declined to choose,
  Dreading the dubious contest for the right,
  . Yet turning each in many a varied light,
A calmer, hopeful feeling soothed his breast,
  Shedding a ray across his mental night
Which ceased not yet the landscape to invest.
For rest was not obtained, but only hope of rest.

XIX.

But hope of rest was grateful.   And it came
  Upon his heart as falls the evening dew
On Summer's thirsty leaves, until the flame
  Of a returning noonday shall renew
  The scorching gaze which all its moisture drew.
No longer now in intellectual pride,
  Seeking to win a self-determined view,
He only seeks a creed that can provide
For his o'erlabored mind, a bold, unwavering guide.

XX.

" Why earth was formed, and why the heavens outspread
  With all the wonders of unbounded space,
Why glow those distant orbs, and wherefore sped
  By hand unseen along their mighty race ?
  And what unchanging purposes embrace
All their stupendous cycles in one whole,
  Binding unerringly each to his place—
Ten thousand suns and systems to one pole,
Round which as single orbs their many orbits roll,

XXI.

" No mind of man can know.   Nor shall I waste
　　My days and years in toil to ascertain
　The inscrutable.   Each being has been placed
　　Where circumstances of themselves explain
　　The duties which the Maker chose to ordain.
　Enough for me thus much of His design
　　To comprehend.   All further quest restrain.
　Follow the dictates of this heart of thine,
　Formed by the heavenly will, its voice must be divine.

XXII.

" The most consoling creed must be the true,
　　As most accordant to the inward voice.
　And for the human race, what all pursue
　　Must be the highest object of its choice,
　　In which its Author bids it to rejoice.
　Shall the Almighty raise His arm to make,
　　And fail in any method He employs?
　Whatever present aspect things may take,
　The works of God are good, and for His glory's sake."

XXIII.

And thus did Alwyn launch into the sea
　·　Of worldly business eagerly to drown
　The craving of his inner life, and free
　　Himself from questions which had settled down
　　Upon his spirit a perpetual frown.
　Where all appeared successfully to fare
　　In search of gold, of office, or renown,
　Might he not hope to find his modest share
　Of temporal success—relief from inward care?

XXIV.

His early years of literary life,
　　Though marked with earnest labor and success,
Had never entered on the fiercer strife
　　Which surges through the gates of business.
　　A young enthusiasm fired him, less
For topics which his rapid pen employed,
　　Than intellectual earnings to possess,
Which earth confers not.　And, although enjoyed,
The work had always in it something of a void.

XXV.

And still, as many see, he only saw
　　The outward show, triumphant march of gain.
Saw not the working of the eternal law,
　　Which by its tense and ever-instant strain
　　Hardens the heart and mollifies the brain—
Saw not beneath the city's upper crust,
　　What misery its inner depths contain,
Knew not how far successful business must,
In being true to self, be inhumanely just.

XXVI.

All things appeared in light of his new creed,
　　Were estimated as they stood that test.
" Whether in speculation or in deed,
　　What makes man happiest must be the best."
　　Such seemed his haven now.　And for the rest—
His intellectual toils had proved but wrecks.
" Men of the world," he said, " seem ever blest
With buoyant hearts, which no such questions vex,
And reach life's aim without a doctrine to perplex."

XXVII.

How many thus, from childhood to the grave,
　Expend their days in varying mistake,
In trying from the ever passing wave
　Of temporal life the spirit's thirst to slake.
　The immaterial in us craves to make
An immaterial and eternal gain.
　We proffer it the present; and awake
To wonder that it seems to crave in vain,
Its voice misunderstood, with all our care and pain.

XXVIII.

Dreading to tread again the dismal coast
　Of rational despair, in which so late
The chart and compass of his course were lost,
　He shuts out speculation and debate
　To meet plain business in its own estate,
To fill its duties, and to bear its load,　　　`
　To gather facts of human life, and wait
On human nature's practicable mode
Of teaching truth, and then rest in the good bestowed.

XXIX.

Knowledge of human nature, worth to man
　The bravest strife by human spirit striven,
Is open deemed to all, who only can
　Behold or listen, as the chance is given,
　To basest men by crawling motives driven.
To know the being in God's image made,
　And filled with an immortal life from heaven,
Must one go down where selfish aims degrade,
And read the solemn lesson by the light of trade?

XXX.

Human nature, form of the ideal,
   The loftiest being by conception traced,
Embodying in itself the living real
    Of all with which ideal life is graced,
    Image of God, though broken and defaced,
Though stained with earth, polluted in the mire,
   Still, that which shall be finally replaced
In holiness, and elevated higher
In majesty divine than the angelic choir:

XXXI.

True human nature, to which men can add
   Nothing but more and better of the same,
When thinking of the attributes of God:
    So vast in apprehension, high in aim,
    So sensitive to favor or to blame;
Whom holiness befits, and moral wrong
   Stains by its touch; and whom it would defame
To praise with highest praises that belong
To any other one earth's habitants among;

XXXII.

Yea, human nature, like all other things,
   Best known where in its best condition found,
Best analyzed when at it purest springs,
    Ought to be studied upon holy ground,
    Where least the bias of false lights surround.
So should we praise its being not the less
   That sins and errors do so much abound.
Not it, but its defects do they express,
For none can sin who are not made for holiness.

   7

XXXIII. ♪

But Alwyn, like the many, thought the gross
    Of human life, the wicked and the low,
Especially denuded of the gloss
    Of artificial covering, must show
    The truth of human nature; and to know
That mystery, in all its breadth and force,
    He rushed with new-enkindled zeal to throw
Himself into the channel of its course,
And seek in human life inquiry's last resource.

XXXIV.

Alas! in rush of business, day by day,
    In nights of care, the waste of all for gain,
So often gathered but to melt away;
    The selfishness, the narrowness, the drain
    Upon the poor, their labors and their pain,
To feed rapacious purses; and the round
    Of deepening crimes and vices, which retain
Both high and low in wretchedness, he found
All nobler aims of life and better feelings drowned.

XXXV.

And in their pleasures what a depth of woe,
    What hearts made desolate and souls destroyed;
What blooming hopes of early life laid low,
    And smiling homes o'erclouded, darkened, void;
    A sacrifice that Moloch might have cloyed,
Offered forever, that the pleasure sought
    By selfish men might daily be enjoyed.
And selfishness itself was sold and bought,
Yet ever in its gains came wretchedly to nought.

XXXVI.

And Alwyn wearied of that bickering life
 Whose fair externals had allured him most,
Its grovelling, toiling, temporalizing strife
 For fleeting pleasures at a lasting cost,
 In which the care-vexed multitude was tossed.
From conscience had he earned no respite,
 And his respect for human nature lost,
And in that loss lost all. The fairest light
Of hope and love and God all vanished from his sight.

XXXVII.

Then while he wept in spirit for the dead,
 And saw the wicked prosper by their wrong,
Amid the ruins of his hopes he said,
 " Alas, and if this wretched human throng
 Be the true lord to whom the zones belong,
The native growth of atoms, then the right
 Is but a fiction ; are they not the strong
Who always rule, in truth and love's despite ?
In vain does Justice plead, when unsustained by might."

XXXVIII.

Blackness of darkness on his spirit fell,
 Extinguishing all purpose, all desire.
What had a chance-created world to tell ?
 What revelation could a heaven inspire
 The necessary birth of frost and fire ?
But wherefore then so passionately pray
 " My God, my God," impelled by something higher
Than all that life and argument can say ?
Poor self-conflicting soul, where shall it find a stay ?

XXXIX.

Nature had taught of nature—nothing more.
　　Philosophy had led to darkest doubt.
Knowledge of human nature only bore
　　The fruit of disappointment.　For without
　　Sight of its loftier ends, the most devout
Philanthropy could only turn to gall.
　　Science alone seemed certain.　But about
Man's origin, his place, and purpose, all
Was silent as the grave, and gloomy as its pall.

XL.

Men may be doubted, and the doubt a gain;
　　But without faith in man there can be none
In God; and they who trust not God remain
　　As infidel to man.　And he alone
　　Who loves his brother man, already known,
Can love the God unseen but by the blest.
　　And faith and love alike have ever grown
From the conviction, natively impressed,
That all things, good'and ill, are ordered for the best.

XLI.

But Alwyn's soul, embittered by the view
　　Of life thus taken, earthy, cold, and sad,
Although a timorous love clung to a few,
　　Revolted from the race, in whom he had
　　Found in the main, the selfish and the bad.
But now necessity had firmly wound
　　Her coils about him; and the life he led,
Though hated, with a spell like that around
The gaming-table, still with chains of iron bound.

XLII.

In surging turmoil and the heat of crowds,
  The inner life withdraws herself from sight,
Shrinks from unsympathizing gaze, and shrouds
  Her form in shades of artificial night.
  As in the smoke and fury-of the fight
The ranks succeed or fail, they know not why,
  So, in the business war, where wrong with right,
Where true and false in desperate conflict vie,
Is not the place to pause with introverted eye.

XLIII.

By him alone, who stands apart and views
  The scene, where cares and passions seethe and boil,
And with a living sympathy pursues
  The tide alike in flow and in recoil,
  Without submitting to their rude turmoil,
Or yielding to their crimes, by him alone
  Who reads his own heart with a patient toil
Is human nature deepest, largest known.
'Tis from above the most impartial light is thrown.

XLIV.

Is there still healing in the lonely wild,
  Where man is but a visitor, and rare ?
Its inspiration filled him when a child ;
  And shall its blessèd agency repair
  The blight which social life has oft to bear ?
The eager spirit half its light relumed
  At thought of days so lovely and so fair.
But Nature had of late for him assumed
Such moods as those to which he had himself been
    doomed.

XLV.

As, seen from Lauterbrunnen's watery vale,
    The sunset glories of the proud Jungfrau
Dissolve by chilling changes ghastly pale,
    As dies the light along the mountain's brow;
    So die the charms which earthly scenes endow,
When of the rays of hopeful fancy shorn;
    And Alwyn fruitless sought in nature now
The fellowship she gave to life's bright morn,
Saw but a pallid corpse—a painted scene outworn.

XLVI.

They who would climb the dazzling mountain's crown,
    Must often pass where avalanches lower,
And from successive summits must go down,
    To climb again, full many a weary hour;
    So the ascent of intellectual power
And truth is oft appalling to the view.
    Gulfs yawn beneath, and precipices tower,
Efforts seem lost 'twere fruitless to renew.
And yet the path of toil and doubt may be the true.

XLVII.

But there was still another, stranger life,
    Lying away behind that conscious scene,
When, all withdrawn from day's harassing strife,
    The soul's unconscious being woke serene.
    Again he rambled o'er the pastures green,
Or lightly scaled the airy mountain wall.
    And he was once again, as he had been
In happy boyhood, ignorant of all
That thinking which had turned the fruit of thought to gall.

XLVIII.

Again the honest earth yielded to him
   The joys of earlier days.   The laughing rill
Played with the grassy lawn along its brim.
   The shadowy forest slumbered on the hill,
   And silent herds did dreamy pastures fill.
Again his limbs did the light winds invest
   Fresh from the gleaming sea.   But all was still,
And, in another light than sunshine drest,
Breathed of a holier realm of purity and rest.

· XLIX.

Then changed the scene, like a dissolving view.
   Earth disappeared.   Distinctly, as if nigh,
One sainted form before his vision grew,
   Well-known and dearly loved ; but far and high,
   On bended knee, in pure and crystal sky,
Which slowly opened round her, and displayed
   Glories of light ineffable, which lie
Where never shades of earthly day invade,
And the angelic ranks round the white throne arrayed.

L.

And still that one beloved on bended knee
   All silent seemed.   And silent all around
The throne of God ; in awful silence He.
   Meanings were uttered, but gave forth no sound.
   Nearer ! O nearer !   But his limbs were bound.
And then words seemed into his heart to pour,
   As having through no outward organ found
Their way, and with deep tenderness implore,
In tones his childhood knew, now heard on earth no more.

LI.

Of him they spake, his dangers still below,
  In doubts, temptations, weaknesses, and sin ;
Pleaded the sad inheritance of woe,
  With which the purest of mankind begin, '
  The grace, which e'en the guiltiest may win,
And earnestly for him that grace besought.
  Alwyn heard no reply ; but felt within
As if upon a beam of glory brought,
A glow of blessedness, the light of holier thought.

LII.

Again the scene dissolved. And as he lay
  By the vast ocean's shore, a face drew near
Out of the darkness, lighted by no ray
  But from itself. Clearer and yet more clear,
  Of heavenly beauty, holy and severe,
Changing to tender, loving, did it seem,
  Till forth stood every feature—O how dear !
But the bliss perished in its own extreme.
He woke, and pondered long the strange ecstatic dream.

LIII.

Within herself the human spirit lives
  A life all separate from what appears.
Though to the world of men her toil she gives,
  'Tis when forgetting them and self she rears
  Her fairest works, weaves her own joys and fears,
And calls around her with most potent sway
  The grand realities of higher spheres,
Which with the self-forgetful soul delay ;
But fleet at slightest touch of consciousness away.

CANTO SEVENTH.

ANALYSIS.

CANTO VII.—Alwyn, after all his studies, in a state of spiritual darkness, desolate, despondent—Pardoners of sin—He returns to his native land—The Minster church—The service—Disappointed, he strolls thoughtfully through the city—Encounters the friend of his youth in destitution—Recital of a lowly Christian's afflictions—They profoundly interest Alwyn's feelings—In the course of continuing to aid his friend, he is led to relieve suffering in others—Becomes acquainted with other persons similarly employed—Learns to hold them in esteem—And to think of Jesus, in whose spirit they profess to act, in a new light—Weighs in his meditations the benevolence and self-sacrifice of Jesus—Through love to His person begins to feel the comfort of confidence in His truth—His meditations swell into a hymn to Christ—Epilogue.

CANTO SEVENTH.

I.

WHAT is there great in all our mortal years,
  In all that can by human skill be known ?
The far-off mighty dwindles as it nears,
  And earnest seekers after truth bemoan
  Their purpose baffled and their hopes o'erthrown.
Ah ! how much labor and exhausting pain,
  What wear of soul, that never can be shown,
Must often be endured to make the gain
Of vital truth, which one bright moment might attain !

II.

Why should so many of transcendent power
  In long unrest their anxious days expend,
Inquiring ever till their latest hour,
  Only to be inquirers at the end—
  Such wealth of thinking to the grave descend,
Without one step of progress on the whole ?
  Must each new life upon itself depend
And leave no help for a succeeding soul
The better to attain the all-desired goal ?

III.

'Twas not that fortune had refused to crown
    Alwyn's industrial toil with competence,
But all life's Spring and Summer now had flown,
    And yet the good he sought at such expense
    Of peace, of human love and severance,
Enlightened not his sad and lone abode.
    All other gains were heartless recompense ;
Yea, all the best by learning's hand bestowed,
While life-exhausting search had failed of peace with
    God.

IV.

Friendships it had not been his care to make.
    To lone pursuits his hermit youth he paid.
And if his lips the words of kindness spake,
    'Twas often that a happy temper made
    It pleasanter than rudeness to be said.
While positive attainments satisfied,
    While life was new and hope her plans arrayed,
While daily study daily joy supplied
He little recked what man or granted or denied.

V.

While fortune smiles and mental stores increase,
    The services of friendship may be brief,
But ill can hermit self-sustain her peace
    With disappointment, failure, unbelief.
    'Tis true, her ear may virtuously be deaf
To hollow phrase of smooth-tongued sons of cant ;
    But to the smile of kindliness, that chief
Of all the gifts of time, 'twere false to vaunt
A disregard or hate, or glory in its want.

VI.

By knowing had he hoped to reach the sure
  System of causes—the eternal bond
Betwixt the work and Maker—the secure
  Step from creation into that beyond,
  Which should to his most solemn wish respond,
And learn with clearness all the aim of prayer,
  And all a sure salvation, which his fond
Devotion craved with ever anxious care.
But every path had ended in " no thoroughfare."

VII.

Could not his soul the wealth of nature fill?
  No charm was lacking in the earth or sky.
And where he lived had Art, with curious skill,
  Long labored, not in vain, to multiply
  All that could bless the heart through ear and eye.
And men and women, in their liquid tongue,
  Confessed their sins, and trusted the reply
Which pardoned them.   And wide, to old and young,
To good and bad, the gates of heaven were open flung.

VIII.

"And wherefore not accept the easy grace,
  Which may be had without this toil of mind?
If some good priest's decision can efface
  The guilt with which my spirit is combined,
  Why not let heart and conscience be resigned?
If there are men who will insist to bear
  Responsibility of such a kind,
Why may I not on them devolve my care,
And leave to them the robe it is their choice to wear?

IX.

But, ah ! the soul that sinneth it shall die.
    One drop of poison may dissolve forever
My hold on life, and all its bonds untie ;
    So must one sin from holy being sever,
    To be rejoined by human effort never.
The laws of nature are the thoughts of God,
    All changeless and unerring.   Like a river
They hasten to their goal.   He bears the load
Of sin who sins ; and he alone must stem the flood.

X.

And whosoever dares to pardon sin
    In others only aggravates his own.
The guilty spirit must retain within
    Its discord with all else that God has done.
    And if aught for that discord can atone
It must be something competent to change
    Creation's nature, to assume the throne
Of monarchy divine, and rearrange
The universe, and causes from effects estrange. "

XI.

As hunted stag, survivor in the chase,
    Seeks wearily the lair from which he rose ;
So wearily did Alwyn now retrace
    His steps, to find at last a sad repose
    Where young success her charms did first disclose.
Not dead to cares of science and of lore,
    A loftier care absorbed his life than those.
And till its calls are met, none evermore
Can to his heart a throb of quickening zeal restore.

XII.

To height sublime a stately fabric rose,
  Solemn, yet light, and in its grandeur fair,
Where studious Art had labored to dispose
  Her ponderous masses with the subtlest care,
  That all might seem to rise and none to bear,
In lightly springing arches, to the eye
  Like gossamer suspended in mid air,
And lines and spires all pointing to the sky,
As if to guide the soul to its true home on high.

XIII.

The giddiest mind the solemn portal awes,
  The worshiper, ere entering, bends low
Upon its threshold stone in reverent pause,
  Till words of prayer in muttered accents flow
  And sprinklings symbolical bestow
A sanctity consistent with the place,
  And then proceeds with motion grave and slow,
With humbled aspect and a muffled pace,
As if 'twere holy ground which those proud aisles em-
    brace.

XIV.

Vast mullioned windows on the assembly threw
  A sober light, like the departing ray
Of Summer's eve, in many tinted hue
  Saddening the lively brilliancy of day.
  And from the walls stood forth, in long array,
Full many a sculptured form of snowy white
  Like angels hovering on their heavenly way,
And dwelling fondly on the pleasing sight,
Ere back to holier scenes they urge their upward flight.

XV.

Lofty and dim the far discernéd roof
  Wrought of the branching arches and the lines
Which indicate in complicated woof,
    The ogive paths, where arc to arc inclines,
    And of the tracery of sculptured vines,
And acorn-bearing oak, appeared to spring
    From native growth, as when·the grove combines
Her leafy arcade of the elm-tree's wing
With all its load of fair retainers clustering.

XVI.

The altar, built of marble and of gold,
  Lit by symbolic tapers, rose on high
Where graceful waving clouds of incense rolled
    Their sweetly-smelling savor to the sky.
    Signs of the death the Saviour chose to die
Stood forth in pride to Calvary unknown.
    And the belovéd Mother bent her eye,
With the benignity a god might own,
On the adoring crowds who knelt before her throne.

XVII.

The ministering priests before the shrine
  Bending in ranks of seemliest array,
The silent multitude, whose souls combine
    Their ceremonial services to pay ;
    The solemn sweetness of the chanted lay,
Lending expression to their thoughts of prayer,
    And the broad music-flood whose upward way
All thoughts, all feelings on its current bare,
With living beauty filled the glad resounding air.

XVIII.

" If aught can please the Lord in worship paid,
    If aught His mind to mercy can dispose,
It must be here." And " Here," the inquirer said,
    " The best that man of God and duty knows
    May I not learn?" But still the question rose,
" Has God required this offering at our hands?
    Can all this pride of human taste unclose
The prison doors of sin, or break her bands?
Who knows that this is what Almighty God demands?"

XIX.

Night was descending as he turned away,
    Deep musing of the pompous worship there,
And of the multitudes who thronged to pay
    Their grand devotions in that incensed air,
    With graceful attitudes and well-toned prayer.
Behind him full the swell of music came,
    From lofty windows poured the tinted glare,
And high the minster rose, as if to claim
Of heaven a hearing in her own proud name.

XX.

Alwyn withdrew with languid steps and slow.
    His early confidence of power was gone.
All goodness seemed to be but hollow show,
    And earnestness possessed by vice alone.
    His heart was cold and passive as a stone.
But jibing fiends ran riot in his brain,
    With bitterest scoff 'on all religion thrown,
And helplessness sought refuge in disdain
Of all that reason proved so helpless to explain.

XXI.

From the enclosed and consecrated ground
  Slowly emerging to the crowded street,
He wandered on in hopelessness profound,
  Nor hearing, seeing, caring where his feet
  Might carry him, so might it be retreat
From bootless thinking. Sounds of rage and woe
  Aroused him from his reverie to greet
Haunts which the outskirts of the city strew,
Like wrecks upon the shore of its cold ebb and flow.

XXII.

He paused a moment thoughtfully, and then
  Resumed his way with now awakened ear
And eye. The lower sufferings of men,
  Who never mounted high enough to fear
  His fears, thus loudly clamorous and near,
Usurped his thoughts, and mixed them with a new
  Train of reflections not more glad or clear.
Till as the thinning city sparser grew
Melting into the country, and the outward view

XXIII.

Peered into dreary darkness cold and void,
  He slowly turned his footsteps to retrace.
And truths, which for a time his mind enjoyed,
  Recurring doubts fast hastening into place
  Might have been suffered wholly to efface,
As others of the kind, but that a low
  Cabin beside him drew his earnest gaze,
Whence issued weeping and the words of woe
Subdued to tenderness such quarters seldom know.

XXIV.

He entered: 'Twas one solitary room,
    But ill-supplied with aught designed to stay
A want of nature. And that squalid gloom
    The humbler haunts of poverty display
    Was deepened by the sorrowful array
Of children weeping for the recent dead,
    From whom a mother had been borne away
That day her body in the dust was laid,
And sleep had their first night of desolation fled.

XXV.

The father stands beside him. And his eye,
    Though sunk with suffering and dim with tears,
Is calm, and though his face is worn, a high
    Composure rests upon it. He appears
    A workman of the humbler class who nears
The even of life. And yet the hoary lock
    Upon his brow was not the gift of years.
Full well the work of years can sorrow mock.
And though the spirit bear, the body owns the shock.

XXVI.

Alwyn, in presence of a sacred grief,
    Felt that the step of stranger ought to pause.
But the fond hope of yielding that relief
    Which, even if nothing could remove the cause,
    Might yet alleviate ; and that which draws
The heart of man to man in times of pain,
    The consciousness of right, the heart's applause,
Soon reassured him, and called up again
Stronger the generous impulse, as its course seemed plain.

XXVII.

But as he looked upon that countenance,
  Worn as it was with suffering, it did seem
As if a recognition warmed the glance,
  Like something half-remembered from a dream ;
  Nay, can it be—is life so brief a gleam—
The Norman whom he loved in early days,
  The Norman of his more mature esteem,
Long lost to sight ?   And is it thus always
That Providence the good of holy men repays ?

XXVIII.

Not words alone answered his kind address,
  But a warm look of heartfelt gratitude,
A joy in grief, which words could not express,
  But found its goal swifter than language could.
  The spirit, long by crushing ills subdued,
Clung to the hand of sympathy.   As friends
  Together in the shade of death they stood,
In that confiding conference which bends
By sympathy of grief to love's most holy ends.

XXIX.

" The Lord is good.   The inflictions of his rod
  Are mixed with mercy.   I should cease to grieve
My need of help when an Almighty God
  Is always near my trials to relieve.
  Yet once it had distressed me to receive
The gift of charity, which now I take
  With humbled feelings, striving to believe,
Though out of hopelessness my bosom ache,
That yet for all, my hands some faint return shall make.

XXX.

' The comforts of the rich we never knew.
　　And yet when first our little home we made,
'Twas full of happiness between us two.
　　For then my work was steady and well paid.
　　And careful hands at home did wisely aid.
So things went on, for many years the same,
　　Full of contentment.　But the rod was laid
Upon me at the last.　For sickness came
And tarried with me long, and left me weak and lame.

XXXI.

" Then business failed.　My labor's worth decreased.
　　Still, we could live, though suffering many a want.
But times grew worse, and all employment ceased.
　　The little saving better days had lent,
　　Though husbanded with care, was quickly spent.
And, though at aught my hands could do I wrought,
　　And had I thus found work had been content,
Such gains were seldom found, and dearly bought.
And many a day passed by when toil was vainly sought.

XXXII.

" Then, one by one, our household things were sold,
　　A scanty meal and seldom to obtain.
Our comfortable home grew bare and cold ;
　　And even there we could not long remain.
　　This hut received us with our little train
Of helpless sufferers.　And I may confess
　　I wept in secret tears of heartfelt pain,
When we had reached this point of our distress.
She murmured not, but bowed with gentle cheerfulness.

XXXIII.

"And when I saw her laboring to give
    An air of comfort to this woeful place,
And when we hardly had the means to live,
    Still striving to maintain a cheerful face,
    I cannot tell my anguish.   But the trace
Of suffering grew deeper.   Week by week
    I saw her health was giving way apace.
She always spoke in words resigned and meek.
But when she slumbered, oft her tears have wet my cheek.

XXXIV.

"The Winter now set in.   And many a day
    I've left her with these little children here,
In cold and hunger, and in the essay
    To earn something, traveled far and near,
    Offering my labor for the humblest cheer,
Yet fruitlessly.   And when the evening came,
    Without the means to wipe away a tear,
Or meet my starving family's silent claim,
Returned to feel a grief no tongue of man can name.

XXXV.

"Sometimes a kinder Providence would aid
    My efforts, yet I could not but behold
What inroads on her health were daily made
    By silent anguish, hunger, damp and cold.
    And when I fondly to my heart would fold
Her wasted form, my bitter tears would flow
    Even as her own, from ills no help consoled.
But most of all that one so good should know
Such destitution and such depths of hopeless woe.

XXXVI.

"But no, not hopeless. That I should not say.
  For hope was to her spirit ever true.
That was a light went with her all the way,
  And nearer to the end the brighter grew,
  And when around her dying bed we drew,
We heard no words of sadness or dismay.
  And in her eye, as seeing clearly through,
And out beyond into a better day,
A world so calm and deep of holy meaning lay."

XXXVII.

The words were strange to Alwyn. "Wherefore such
  A wondrous gratitude to the Most High,
Which not those sorest sufferings could touch?
  And why with such a heart should this man lie
  Under the wrath which passes others by?"
He would have said. But such an hour must be
  Sacred to feelings which another eye
Should not in their outgoing lightly see.
He hastened his adieu to leave the full heart free.

XXXVIII.

But often did he tread the path again
  To that low cabin. For in doing good,
In kindly minist'ring to want and pain,
  Had he discovered peace, which never could
  Be won from Learning in her holiest mood.
A bliss which all might share. And yet, alas!
  How ill so rich a vein is understood,
The heart's best treasures trodden like the grass
By pleasure-seeking crowds, who lose the good they pass.

XXXIX.

Of rectitude in such a course, or of
    The pleasure he awakened or enjoyed
He listened not for doubts, nor for the scoff
    Which callous unbelief might have employed.
    However his reflections were annoyed
With questionings, his actions were most clear.
    And from that dreary, intellectual void—
Unbroken save by consciousness of fear—
The task which could relieve was to his spirit dear.

XL.

A page of life had opened to his mind,
    Which his philosophy had never taught,
And though to much his reason yet was blind,
    With lessons of a high instruction fraught,
    Not all in one perusal to be caught.
The plans of God are of such vast extent
    As not to be embraced by human thought
Without long patience and a spirit bent
To study all the ways of their development.

XLI.

And, day by day, the duty self-imposed,
    But from an impulse he would not gainsay,
A spring of intellectual health disclosed.
    The approving thought of something done to stay
    The course of suffering, served to allay
Despondency which had of late imbued
    The current of his reasonings. The array
Of argument, which fair embattled stood
Against existence fled before one act of good.

XLII.

But wherefrom came this practical belief
  In the reality of all these deeds ?
Had he not followed Reason as his chief,
  And reached the end to which that chieftain leads,
  Annihilation of all hopes and creeds?
Then wherein can the evidence consist
  From which a confidence so full proceeds?
He feels an independent power enlist
His energies ere Doubt can rally to resist—

XLIII.

A power as native to the human heart,
  As sovereign, too, as Reason's proudest reign,
In the economy of life whose part
  Is to supply what Reason must restrain—
  The sole producer in the mind's domain,
Who unobtrusively forever toils;
  And, even when her crafty rival's chain
Is wound about her limbs, who quietly foils
His labored skill in fence, and carries off the spoils.

XLIV.

Instinctive faith—native impulsive trust—
  In all the impressions by the sense conveyed,
As broad realities of being, must
  Be prior to all reasoning, and laid
  As law imperative to be obeyed
By all who think aright.   New life awoke
  Within him as he saw.   No more dismayed,
He listened to the language nature spoke,
And on his soul again the light of knowledge broke.

8

XLV.

'Twas not that any doubt had been dispelled,
For none had yet been solved. But he had found
In the dark waters which around him swelled,
At last a footing upon solid ground.
He sinks no more, though gloomy depths surround.
His work of charity, which daily sought
From love of man, not truth, became a sound
Instructor in philosophy, and taught,
Despite the skeptic's creed, the highest things of thought.

XLVI.

And often, too, with Norman as his guide,
New realms of destitution he explored,
For suffering with bounty to provide
With ever open hand and kindly word,
And where his own means failed him, to record
Its worthy objects for benevolence,
And to neglected industry afford
The path of labor and its recompense,
Became to him a joy, a new-discovered sense.

XLVII.

And then at times, as on his couch he lay
And sleep delayed before the healthful cares
Which with so warm an interest filled his day,
He thought of Christ, and of His midnight prayers,
And how He loved the poor and their affairs
Took to His bosom ; and the toils and death
To which He gave Himself to lighten theirs.
And learned to know through more of love than faith
The self-denying man—the man of Nazareth.

XLVIII.

And it did seem to him that he had found
  Both men and women, who from door to door
Carried their works of charity around
  Among the lowly dwellings of the poor,
  Who were like Jesus—like in that they wore
No badge of goodness, and that self-denied, ·
  With meekness the perversities they bore
Of those to whom their charities applied,
In mercy's mighty power o'ermastering hate and pride.

XLIX.

And then his wondrous doctrine of love
  Stood forth in that new light with meaning new.
It was the chain descending from above,
  Which sentient being to one centre drew—
  God's free necessity—a law of true
Compassion, not to be confined within
  Love to the lovely, whose best gains accrue
To those, whom otherwise no love could win,
The poor, debased, and outcast children of sin.

L.

It rose before him as the sovereign good
  The mystery of human happiness—
Nor human only. "Is there aught that could
  The purest of angelic natures bless
  If destitute of love? Or to express
The truth in heaven's own language, God is love ;
  Nor to be good and blessed can be less.
And who for suffering mortals ever strove
Like Christ to plant on earth the exotic from above?

LI.

" Then Christ historical, as God or man,
    Or both united, is alone the true
  Messiah of our happiness, who can
    Capacity for holy love renew.
    To Him the heart of suffering man is due.
  Yea, Blessed Master, whatsoe'er the creeds
    Define of Thee, I would repose my view
  Upon Thy truth of love sustained by deeds,
  Thine eye that weeps for sin, Thy yearning heart that
      bleeds.

LII.

" Nor His the touch of human life to shun,
    To seek in purity a plea for pride.
  His tenderest words, His mightiest works, begun
    In fierce temptation, were full oft applied
    To publican and sinner, nor denied
  To Magdalene repentant, whom the rest
    Of her own gentle sex would spurn aside.
  More than unsoiled, outgoing virtue bless'd
  Where'er His footsteps moved, and every ill repress'd.

LIII.

" And who shall estimate the weight of woe
    The gospel of that holy One hath stayed,
  How it hath soothed the mourner, lit the glow
    Of hope, where hope had long ago been dead,
    Hath filled the poor with gladness, and arrayed
  The meek with power, and deem it not a plan
    For man's salvation, and most wisely laid,
  Or doubt that He, with whom the work began,
  In whose rich love it sprang, was man—yet more than
      man ?

LIV.

" A gentle heart with tenderness o'erflowing,
  With sympathy for every human ill,
An intellect of boundless grasp, all-knowing,
  Discerning to the very depths of will,
  Which soared above all reach of human skill,
Whose wisdom none could fathom, and whose words
  Remain prolific of high meaning still ;
Whose simplest lesson more of truth affords
Than all that ethic lore of Grecian sage records.

LV.

" A man who without learning or ripe years,
  Poor, and with lowly rank to weigh him down,
Who as an humble peasant youth appears
  Above philosophers of old renown ;
  Yea, teaching solemn verities unknown
To Socrates and Plato, after all
  Wherewith old age the work of lore could crown—
A man who erred not in the great or small,
Transcends all human greatness since the primal fall.

LVI.

" To whom shall he be likened ?   To the wise,
  The learnéd, or the gifted, or the good ?
To heroes of ambition and emprise ?
  To men who have persuaded or subdued,
  And bent the will of nations to their mood ?
It dawns upon us in a light divine,
  The mighty stature at which Jesus stood
Above all other men in power benign,
In grandeur of effect and wisdom of design."

LVII.

As meditating thus one night he lay,
  And many a tranquil hour of late had sped
In thoughts that held such unpretending sway,
  These words of Jesus came into his head,
  With light and comfort through his spirit shed,
" That God so loved the world." It was not new ;
  A hundred times had he that language read ;
But now a meaning rose upon his view,
- Which evidenced itself triumphantly as true.

LVIII.

" God loved the world—so loved it that He gave
  His well belovéd Son to human grief,
To human toil, to suffering and the grave,
  That He, their mighty Substitute and Chief,
  From all their ills procuring full relief,
Might make them partners in his blest abode.
  God loved the world ! Whate'er of unbelief
May touch the fact, the doctrine is a broad,
A tender, godlike offspring of the heart of God.

LIX.

" What heathen priest, what brain of sinful man
  Could ever dream—did ever dare to dream
That the Almighty and most Holy One
  Loves sinners, all unlovely as they seem
  To one another, and must be to Him
Abhorring sin, and takes their guilt away ?
  Ah ! This is gospel—in itself a beam
Of heavenly light, it signals brighter day,
On which no night shall fall, nor saddening cloud delay.

LX.

" Christ is the truth.   The truth in Him alone
  Stoops to the level of poor human thought.
The primal truth, whose central radiance shone
  Upon the birth of time, is ever fraught
  With all that time contains.   And He who wrought
Creation's work, is truth as well as might.
  And what He gave His work, His gospel taught—
The truth which shows all other truth aright,
And brings heaven, life and immortality to light.

LXI.

" Self-humbled Son of God, atoning lamb,
  Who once for men descended from Thy throne,
How shall I praise Thee, sinful as I am,
  All holy as Thou art ?   Through Thee alone
  Is God to man in love and mercy known.
In Thy commands all duty lies enshrined,
  From beauty's full perfection hast Thou shone,
Thyself more fair than form of human kind.
And Thou alone hast peace to calm the troubled mind.

LXII.

." How ill we comprehend Thy Word of life,
  And what laborious helplessness we prove,
What wars we wage, what unavailing strife
  Within our souls to take Thy hand of love.
  Not by the path of learning must they move,
Not by the light of human wisdom see,
  Who would secure the wisdom from above.
Humbler the way, and briefer far must be—
Faith of the docile heart, which rests alone on Thee.

LXIII.

" How lofty Thy humility became,
    Without reserve for earthly honors made.
No title of their gift adorned Thy name,
    No party lines along the nation spread
    Lent to Thy work their adventitious aid.
Lowly Thy birth among the lowliest poor,
    Lowly Thy life, and on Thy people's head
Rested the shade of fortune most obscure.
And Galilee had learned in patience to endure.

LXIV.

" And yet what transformations have been wrought
    By Thy so humble life upon mankind ;
Hard-hearted men made tender, word and thought,
    The once polluted chaste, the coarse refined,
    The timid valiant, and the wavering mind
Fixed to one lofty purpose.   That which sums
    Up all the best in human life designed,
And all the grace that blesses happiest homes
Spring up along the path by which Thy mercy comes.

LXV.

" For Thee has Genius wreathed the bay and palm,
    For Thee the sweetest harps on earth been strung,
Expectant harmonies of Hebrew psalm,
    And pre-ordained prophetic pæons sung.
    For Thee, before Thy wondrous birth, Thy young
And virgin mother raised the adoring strain.
    For Thee the gates of heaven were open flung,
And hymning angels, in long choral train,
Issued with glorious song to hail Thy earthly reign.

LXVI.

" A chorus worthy of a heavenly choir,
   A hymn to go resounding through all time,
Announced Thy birth in spirit of a higher
   Degree of being, and a loftier clime.
   Thy Life laborious, suffering, yet sublime,
In singleness, severity of aim,
   Though brief, and closed in early manhood's prime,
Beyond all measure of mere mortal fame,
An epic grander far than mind of man could frame.

LXVII.

" And ever since, Thy love, and living faith
   In Thee have filled believing souls with light,
Their life with hopeful labor, and their death
   With joy of hope, then dawning into sight.
   To Thee the prisoners, at dead of night,
Prayed and sang praises. And the lowly few,
   Shunning offence to heathen law or might,
Ere busy worldlings woke, would press the dew
To meet in prayer with those whose equal love they
      knew,

LXVIII.

" And sing a hymn to Christ. And still of Thee
   The lonely singers in the long, drear night
Of error chanted sad, but lovingly.
   And, as the Holy Spirit, in despite
   Of jangling discords, tuned the heart aright,
Telling self-tortured men of glad reward,
   Spreading all heaven to Damian's ravished sight,
And speaking love, where earthly love was barred,
To the worn mind and gentle heart of Saint Bernard.

LXIX.

" The tongue of Greece revived again in Thee,
  For Thee Old Latin vowed her latest strains.
And first of recent powers to issue free
  From mediæval and barbaric chains
  The harp that for the Lord its art retains.
And civil culture waking from the dead,
  Did to Thy glory pay her earliest gains,
In arts and learning on Thy gospel fed,
Whence a new morning's dawn along the nations spread.

XLX.

" And to the race of man, immersed in sin,
  Enslaved to its imperious control,
Harassed by foes without, and foes within,
  As if a leaguered nature were the whole
  Inheritance of every human soul,
And woe were all that Nature had to give,
  Christ has appointed a triumphant goal,
And by His sovereign grace reformative,
Has rendered human lifé a glorious life to live.

LXXI.

" O Nature, in the light of heavenly love,
  How rise thy beauties more divinely fair,
The light comes more benignly from above,
  And inspiration fills the buoyant air,
  More charming tints thý hills and valleys wear.
For God now meets me tenderly among
  The scenes to which I also kindred bear.
Would that His worship I might aye prolong
With love's pure incense breathed from censer of sweet
    song."

EPILOGUE.

FAIN would my lay, belovéd, once again
   Revert to thee—for thee it woke alone—
With praise to thee would close its latest strain,
   Though never more to hear the loving tone
   Of thy melodious voice the tribute own,
Nor see the smile thy radiant cheek illume.
   The garland wove not many days agone,
In the fond hope to crown thy ripened bloom,
With heavy heart I bring, and lay it on thy tomb.

NOTES.

CANTO II. *Stanza* 5.—Æolico-Ionian. By this phrase I do not mean to imply that Epic Greek was composed of Æolic and Ionic ; but that it is most characteristically marked by features afterwards appropriated by those dialects.

Stanza 14.—Romance did not prosper in subsequent classic times. It is therefore the more remarkable that the Odyssey is one of the purest specimens of romance in existence.

Stanza 17.—Great as the loss suffered by all departments of ancient literature, in crossing the desert of the Middle Ages, perhaps none is more to be regretted than that which has befallen Greek Lyric poetry. Its remains glow with natural feeling, and fill the imagination with the suggestive beauty which pertains to fragments of perfected art.

Stanza 31.—Horace, Odes I. 34.

CANTO III. *Stanza* 38.—Some of the imagery in this stanza was taken from an anonymous book of travels called " Rome in the Nineteenth Century."

Stanza 57.—For the American Revolution the people were prepared by a deep sense of wrong inflicted on them ; but the words of Patrick Henry nerved them for the crisis.

www.ingramcontent.com/pod-product-compliance
Lightning Source LLC
Chambersburg PA
CBHW030609040726
47497CB00008B/2912